SHERIFF

by
MAGGIE CARPENTER

Cover Design
https://fantasiafrogdesigns.wordpress.com/
Cover Image
Rob Lang
Visit Maggie Carpenter
http://www.MaggieCarpenter.com
https://www.facebook.com/MaggieCarpenterWriter

CHAPTER ONE

Her back pressed against the wall of the building, her heart pounding and her panic rising, Violet Parker tried to calm her desperate breathing. The unnerving high-pitched shrill of the police whistles were drawing closer. If she was caught it would mean prison, and even worse, an interrogation by the dreaded Detective Connelly. At the end of the alley was a pile of junk, and for a moment she considered hiding beneath it, but it was a foolish notion. The constables would surely hunt through it and she'd end up a smelly mess for no good reason.

"What can I do?" she muttered frantically. "There must be..."

Then it came to her. An idea so outlandish it would have to work.

Running down the short narrow lane she hurriedly unbuttoned her blouse and pulled it off, then removing her skirt she rolled them together, and stuffed them under a crate. Her reddish-brown hair was pinned under a pink bonnet, and hastily removing it, she took away the hairpins letting her long locks spill around her shoulders.

But her bag.

Her precious bag.

It didn't just contain her clothes and personal items, but the only money she had in the world. Dashing to the opposite side of the mess, she hurriedly hid it under a pile of boxes.

The whistles grew louder!

The police were perilously close.

Throwing herself on the ground, she winced as she hit the rough dirt, but there was no time to think about the sharp pain throbbing through her elbow. Sprawled on the earth in her undergarments she closed her eyes and waited to be found.

"HEY! OVER HERE!" she heard a male voice shout.

She'd made it with seconds to spare.

"Miss, Miss, are you all right?"

Opening her eyes, Violet saw a worried young constable crouched beside her. Wanting to fluster him further she rolled on her back, exposing her ample cleavage. It had the desired effect. He blushed beet red.

"A woman, she attacked me," Violet whimpered, covering her chest with her arms in feigned shyness. "Dear Lord, I'm so embarrassed."

"Don't you worry," he said urgently, hastily unbuttoning his jacket. "You're safe now."

As he laid the jacket over her she spied two more officers marching down the alley. Slowly sitting up, she covertly scrutinized them as she wrapped the coat around her. They didn't look familiar and she let out a breath of relief. One was another young constable, but the other was mature. She'd need to be careful with him.

"Easy, ma'am," the older man said, pushing the wide-eyed youth out of the way. "Are you all right?"

"I think so, just my elbow. I'm so embarrassed," she repeated, looking at him woefully.

"May I see?"

"Uh, all right, I suppose," she murmured, in the best timid voice she could muster.

Stretching out her arm from under the jacket, she was surprised by the injury. It looked worse than it felt. The skin had been ripped away, and blood was oozing from the nasty gash.

"That will hurt for a bit, but you'll be okay," the policeman said reassuringly and with the slightest hint of an Irish accent. "Tell me what happened."

"I was just walking down the street minding my own business when this woman suddenly shoved me into this alley. She even had a gun. I was so scared. She made me take off my dress, then she put it on right in front of me. Not over her own clothes, I didn't mean that. Oh, dear, I'm sorry, I'm just so upset. She pushed me to the ground then climbed over that wall."

"What was she wearing?"

"A pink bonnet, a white blouse and a grey skirt. She stuffed them under the mess over there by that crate. What am I going to do? She didn't just rob me of my clothing, she took my purse as well," Violet lamented, tears beginning to dribble down her cheeks. "How will I get home?"

"What color was your dress?"

"Powder blue with pink flowers, and it had lace around the waist. It was one of my favorites," she mumbled, her face crinkling in despair, then dropping her head into her hands she began to sob.

"Take a breath. We're here now. Tell me your name."

"Marigold," Violet lied, sniffling as she raised her head. "Marigold Adams. I'm sorry, I don't mean to be so upset."

"It's understandable, ma'am, and you're right, we can't have you wandering around the streets, uh, like you are. How would you feel about wearing that woman's clothes just long enough to get you out of here?"

"I, uh, I suppose."

"Griffin," he said sharply, turning to the young constable standing behind him. "Dig them out, and be quick about it. I need to make sure everyone knows to look for a woman wearing a blue dress with pink flowers."

"Yes, sir."

"Try not to worry," he said warmly, turning back to her. "I'm sure we'll catch this woman and get your purse."

"Thank you for helping me."

"Just doing my job."

"It's going to feel strange putting on her things. Your men won't mistake me for her, will they?"

"I'll have Constable Griffin escort you home so you can change, then you'll have to come down to the station and give us a statement."

"I'll be happy to, but yes, I definitely need to clean up and change."

"Tell me, Marigold, was the woman carrying a bag?"

"She was. She put my purse in it. I don't know how she made it over the wall with that big thing. Funny though..."

"What's that?"

"She looked familiar."

"You've seen her before?"

"I think so."

"Where?"

"I have a cousin who lives on the East side of town. She's poorly, I visit her quite often and I could swear I've seen that woman there."

"Why do you think you're mistaken?"

"It's not a very nice area, Sergeant. You are a sergeant, right? I thought that's what I heard."

"Yes, I'm a sergeant. What you were saying about where you saw her?"

"Folk from there don't generally come to this part of town."

"I think there's a very good chance that's exactly where that woman lives. You've been a big help."

"I have?"

"Excuse me," the young constable said stepping forward. "Here are the clothes. They're not too bad."

"All right, Marigold, you get on home and I might see you at the station house later. If I'm not there the constable will take you to see Detective Connelly. He's the one you'll need to speak with."

"Sergeant, who is this woman?" Violet asked innocently. "Why did she attack me?"

"Her name is Violet Parker. The detective has been after her for some time."

"What has she done?"

"What hasn't she done, more like?" Griffin piped up. "There isn't an area of this city she hasn't conned someone. Today she confused a butcher exchanging money and walked away with—"

"That's enough, Griffin," the sergeant said sternly as he straightened up. "See this young lady home then go back to the station. Goodbye, Marigold."

"Goodbye, Sergeant, and thank you again."

"Here you are," Griffin said, awkwardly handing Violet the skirt and blouse as his sergeant marched away. "I hope they fit."

"Would you mind terribly standing guard at the end of the alley? I'd die if someone were to see me getting dressed."

"Yes, of course. I should have thought of that myself."

"It might take me a while. I'm still a bit shaky."

"Take all the time you need. You join me when you're ready."

"Thank you ever so much. I never knew what lovely policemen we have here."

"Thank you, ma'am."

"Marigold. You can call me Marigold," she twinkled at him. "What's your name?"

"Uh, George. George Griffin."

"Very nice to meet you, George. So, will you go to the end of the alley?"

"What? Oh, yes. Sorry. As I said, take your time."

"Thank you, George. See you in a few minutes, and when we get back to my place I'll make you some coffee. Is that all right? You being on duty, I mean."

"As long as we don't tell," he said with a happy grin.

"Not a soul."

"Right, well then, I'll just go on up to the street."

"No peeking!"

"I wouldn't dream of it, Marigold."

CHAPTER TWO

Violet waited until he was well on his way before hurriedly dressing, then retrieving her bag she carefully clambered up the mess of junk and peered over the wall. On the other side was a children's playground with not a soul in sight, but it was a long drop. She'd have to remove her shoes to land safely.

Looking over her shoulder she saw Griffin standing straight and tall with his hands behind his back. She almost felt sorry for him, but she had no time for guilt. Dropping her bag, she turned her attention to her feet. Though precariously balanced she managed to remove her fashionable boots and toss them over, then straddling the narrow top, she swung one leg down, and gripping the edge, followed it with the other and let go.

Though she tumbled as she landed, she was unhurt, and quickly pulled on her boots, grabbed her bag, and walked swiftly across the play-ground.

She'd been on her way to a stage-coach office when she'd decided to do a last-minute swindle for some extra cash. To her chagrin the butcher realized what was happening and tried to detain her. She'd managed to escape his grasp, but he'd run out of the store and raised the alarm.

"Why did I do it?" she grumbled. "If nothing else it was a sign I need to get out of there, that's for sure."

As she turned down the main road in the direction of the stagecoach office she saw no sign of police officers. They'd be well on their way to her old neighborhood, but she still had to change clothes. The young constable wouldn't stay at his post much longer, then the jig would be up. Spying a dress shop a little further ahead, she quickened her pace, and pushing through the store door she could see it would be expensive. It didn't surprise her. It was an upmarket area.

"Good afternoon," the saleswoman said, eyeing her up and down as she approached.

"You must forgive me. I'm in a terrible state," Violet began, feigning an upscale East Coast accent. "I'm afraid I just had a frightful argument with my husband. We're here from New York."

"New York?"

"Yes, he's a surgeon. He rather likes the idea of moving to this new frontier. That's what San Francisco is called in our circles. The New Frontier. Anyway, there's a new hospital being built here and he's come to speak to the men in charge about heading up their surgical department."

"My goodness. I'm well aware of that hospital. Everyone is. How exciting."

"I suppose it is, except we had a frightful argument and I threw my wedding ring at him. I was so upset I tossed a few things into this bag and left, and now, well, look at the state of me. I was so flustered I tripped as I was hurrying away from the hotel. I have no intention of leaving him. I just wanted to scare him, but now I've hurt my arm. See the blood coming through the material?"

"That's just terrible. I have some bandages in the back. You must let me help you."

"That's very kind of you, but it's probably not as bad as it looks. The problem is, everything in my bag will be crumpled as well, and I cannot abide looking like this. I was planning on visiting Gump's but I'd be embarrassed walking in dressed as I am."

"I'm sure I can find something that will be suitable."

"You do have a lovely shop, but I'm afraid I left with very little money. Silly me! Would you be willing to send a bill? We're staying at the Palace Hotel, though I have no intention of going back there until the sun begins to set. Let him stew, I say! Men!"

"I'm, uh, not sure the owner would approve."

"You're not the owner? Is the owner available?"

"I'm afraid not. He doesn't come here very often. I'm the manager."

"I certainly wouldn't want to get you into any trouble...sorry, I didn't catch your name."

"Mildred. Mildred Thomas."

"How do you do. I'm Emily O'Connor. My husband is Harold O'Connor. You've no doubt heard of O'Connor Tonic?"

"That's your husband?"

"Yes, in fact I have some of the mixture with me. I never go anywhere without it. It's such a cure-all."

"I have a suggestion," Mildred said, lowering her voice. "We'll find you something and you can sign for it. That way if Mr. Martin, that's the owner, if he says anything I can say you guaranteed payment. Of course by the time he shows up your husband will have taken care of the matter. I just need it in case Mr. Martin shows up unexpectedly. Would you do that?"

"Of course I will. Thank you, Mildred, and you must join us for dinner one night this week. I insist, and I'll make sure Harold lets me come back here to buy more of your lovely outfits."

"That would be wonderful, Emily. Thank you."

"Thank *you*, Mildred. It's the least I can do. Unfortunately this sort of thing happens when we travel. He becomes irritable when he's tired. He was an absolute bear for days when we arrived in London."

"You've been to London?"

"Lovely place, then we went on to Paris. Divine, though I don't speak French so it was a bit difficult at times."

"I have a new dress in from Paris. Let me show it to you. I know you'll love it."

Fifteen minutes later, wearing a stylish new blouse and skirt, Violet left the store and hurried to the stage coach office to board the first departing carriage. She didn't care where it was headed, she just needed to exit

San Francisco. The city had been good to her, but the dastardly Detective Connelly had been pursuing her for almost two years, and after a recent narrow escape she couldn't risk staying.

Arriving at the depot, she entered carrying herself with the aplomb and attitude to match her expensive new clothes, and approaching the counter she had to suppress a grin. The mature clerk perked up the moment he saw her.

"May I help you?"

"When is your next coach departing and where is it going?"

"In about ten minutes, and it's headed south."

"How far south?"

"The last stop is a small town called Brownsville."

"Brownsville," she said thoughtfully, the name conjuring up images of cactus and desert. "Do you know anything about it?"

"It started with a gold mine but the gold ran out. Now it's mostly ranchers and such like. Never been there but I've heard good things."

"So it's not a desert."

"Oh, no, it's not a desert. Not like Arizona. Are you looking for a place to take a vacation?"

"Not exactly," she replied, looking at him with a pained expression. "I'm leaving my husband. I can't take it anymore. I want to go as far as the coach can take me."

"Are you sure? That's a long, difficult journey for a young lady."

"Nothing could be more difficult than being with that man a single second longer. He shoved me to the ground. Look what he did to my arm," she said woefully, pulling up the loose sleeve of her new blouse.

"That's terrible. You should go to the police."

"I can't. He has friends on the force. Please, sir, if anyone comes in here asking after me, I beg you, don't tell them I've been here or where I'm going."

"Don't you worry. Your secret is safe with me, Mrs...?"

"I won't mention my name. That way you won't have to lie."

"Aren't you a clever lass."

"Thank you. I just want to be in a nice quiet place for a while, a place I can gather my thoughts and feel safe."

"I understand."

"I don't have much money on me. I hope the fare isn't too expensive."

"I have a daughter about your age, and I'd like to think a stranger would help her if she ever found herself in a pickle like you. Here, take this ticket. We'll just keep it between ourselves. If anyone asks I can honestly say I didn't sell any tickets to any pretty young ladies."

"Oh, my goodness. Thank you. You're so kind."

"Best hurry. It'll be leaving soon."

A short time later, as the carriage rolled through the city streets, Violet let out a long, relieved sigh. She genuinely craved a quiet place to live, and a small town sounded heavenly. All she wanted was to meet a decent man, marry him and have precious babies.

"Is that too much to ask?" she murmured. "Dear Lord, I hope not."

CHAPTER THREE

Sheriff Cooper Dalton marched down the dusty street, and nearing the brawling hotheads he removed his gun from his holster. The bystanders egging them on immediately fell away, but the fighters weren't yet aware of his presence. It was much easier attracting attention firing a gun in the air than yelling, and raising his pistol he pulled the trigger. As the shot rang out, the two boys jumped away from each other and stared around in fright.

"What the heck do you think you're doin'?" Cooper demanded. "You know I don't allow fightin' in the streets."

"Charlie started it!" the smaller of the two young men exclaimed. "He said some things."

"Start walkin! And I mean both of you!"

"But, Sheriff—"

"Jeb, if you and Charlie don't start walkin' to my jailhouse by the time I finish talkin' it'll be two nights, not just one, and I won't have supper brought in."

"Dagnabbit, Charlie," Jeb muttered as he shuffled his feet forward. "See what you've done?"

"Ain't my fault," Charlie retorted. "You could've walked away."

Cooper knew it was just high spirits. Nature demanded they grow into men and fighting was part of the process, but that didn't mean he could let it lie. He considered Brownsville his town. He cared about its folk, and it was his responsibility to keep law and order.

"Sheriff?"

"Yeah, Jeb?"

"Will you let ma know? She'll worry."

"You're such a baby," Charlie quipped. "Worried about your ma."

"Charlie Johnson! Are you sayin' you don't care about your mother?" Cooper asked brusquely, slapping him on the back of his head.

"Ow! What'd ya do that for?"

"She's a good woman. You should be ashamed sayin' somethin' like that. You want me tellin' her you don't give two hoots?"

"No! I do. A lot."

"Then watch your mouth boy. You speak about your mother with respect. You don't, you'll have me to answer to."

"Yes, sir."

Charlie had sounded deferential and Cooper believed he'd been sincere.

"We're really sorry, Sheriff," Jeb said earnestly as they walked inside the sheriff's office. "It won't happen again."

"Get on through that door to the cells," Cooper ordered, "and you'd best remember if you're foolish enough to start brawlin' again, you'll be in the cages for a week. What were you fightin' about?"

"Molly Harris," Jeb replied as Cooper bustled them into the same cell.

"What about Molly Harris?"

"Charlie said something I didn't like."

"Defendin' a woman's honor," Cooper chuckled. "There's nothin' more likely to get you into trouble than that. What'd you say, Charlie?"

"Nothin'."

"I'll ask you again and you'd best answer. What'd you say?"

"I, uh, I said I'd like to, uh..."

"Go on."

"Rub my face in her titties. She's got real big ones."

"Did you say that out loud?"

"Not too loud."

"You shouldn't have said it at all," Jeb barked angrily. "She's a nice girl and you can't talk about her that way."

"That's just cos you're sweet on her," Charlie shot back.

"I reckon Jeb's right," Cooper declared. "We all like the ladies, but you've gotta learn when you can speak your mind, and when to keep your mouth shut. If Molly's pa got wind of you sayin' somethin' like that he'd whip your ass, and he'd be right to do it."

"Yes, Sheriff."

"You two make peace. I have no problem keepin' you as long as it takes." Studying their faces he knew they wouldn't give him any trouble, but as he returned to his office a frown crossed his brow. He was worried about Charlie. The lad was showing a wild streak, and he was growing into a brawny man. Pretty soon he'd be a force to be reckoned with. His rebellious side needed to be nipped in the bud, and Cooper made a mental note to speak to his father. Zeke Johnson was one of the most successful ranchers in the area. He had four strapping boys, all of them respectful and hard working. Charlie was the youngest, and Cooper was confident Zeke could rein his son in.

He glanced up at the clock on the wall. The stagecoach should be arriving soon, and he always made sure he was there when the passengers stepped out. Not only did he like to welcome those returning, he made it a point to size up any new arrivals. He kept up to date with the wanted notices, though he'd been known to offer second chances to those he believed deserving.

He'd once been a hired gun with the reputation of being one of the fastest and sharpest shooters in the West. It had even been rumored he was related to the famous Dalton gang. If he was, he had no sure knowledge of it, but with the guidance of a strong-minded lawman he had turned his life around. It was why he'd chosen to become a sheriff. Inspired by his mentor he now used his God-given talents for good.

Heading out of his office he wandered down Main Street to the stagecoach depot. It was a one room cabin manned three hours a day by Tim Hardy, who also owned the livery stable. Everyone knew to drop off their mail or packages between 1 and 4 p.m. The coaches generally arrived during those three hours.

"Morning, Sheriff."

"Mornin', Hannah," he said, smiling at one of the many young ladies who graced the town.

"Off to meet the stagecoach?"

"Yep."

She gazed at him longingly, trying to keep her eyes off his bare chest. He wore only his trousers and boots when it was hot. Early on it had caused a stir, but the town was now used to their shirtless sheriff, and on blistering summer days it wasn't uncommon to see a few other men follow his example.

"Sure is warm today," she murmured. "Maybe I should stop by the general store and get some lemonade. Would you care for any?"

Cooper knew she had a crush on him and was hoping he'd accept her offer, but Cooper had no intention of sharing his time with her or any other female. The last thing he wanted or needed was the complication of a woman in his life. He was already married to his job.

"I'll be seein' you," he said politely, touching his hat. "My best to your folks."

"Um, Sheriff."

"Yes, Hannah."

"Maybe you could stop by for a visit one of these days."

"If I have a reason to."

"Oh, but, uh—"

"Excuse me, Hannah, there's the coach. You have a nice day."

As he walked briskly forward he could feel her eyes on his back. He didn't like disappointing anyone, but Hannah had already known what he'd say. Everyone was aware of his feelings about stepping out with a lady on his arm, but he had to admire her pluck.

The passengers were climbing out of the carriage, and he hurried forward to greet Pearl Beasley. She'd been away for a month visiting relatives.

"Hello, Sheriff. My, oh, my, it's nice to be home."

"How's your family?"

"Very well, but Silas, that's my older brother, he's limping, poor man. Took a tumble from his fresh young filly on a cattle run, but he'll be fine. Where is that son of mine?"

"I think that's him runnin' down the street."

"It sure is. Bye, Sheriff."

"Bye, Pearl."

As they'd been speaking he'd caught sight of the three remaining passengers. Two were local men who'd been gold-mining, but the woman waiting for the driver to get her bag was a stranger. A very attractive stranger.

"Welcome to Brownsville," he said warmly, stepping up to meet her. "I'm the Sheriff. My name's Cooper Dalton, but most folks just call me Sheriff."

The young woman was staring up at the husky driver who now had her luggage, but as she turned around, Cooper felt a strange sensation ripple through his body.

Not unpleasant, but certainly unfamiliar.

CHAPTER FOUR

Staring at the half-naked, handsome man in front of her, it took a moment for Violet to compose herself, but quickly breaking into a warm smile, she extended her hand.

"Nice to meet you, Sheriff. My name is Rose Hamilton."

"Here you go ma'am," the driver said, placing the bag next to her. "It's been real nice havin' you."

"That's very kind of you, and thank you for all your help along the way."

"Like I said, pleasure was all mine. I'm gonna take the horses down to the livery then head on over to the saloon. If you feel like a cool drink you're welcome to join me. Howdy, Sheriff."

"Howdy, Duke."

"I hope I'll be seein' you," the driver continued.

"Possibly," Violet answered, though now completely distracted by the rippling muscles of the shirtless sheriff.

"Let me carry this for you," he suddenly offered. "Do you have a place to stay or are you visitin' relatives?"

"I'm here because I want to live in a nice quiet town," she replied, trying to will away the hot blush crossing her face. "I have no idea where I'll be laying my head."

"I'll take you over to Ruby Elwood's boarding house. She keeps things orderly and I can attest to her cookin'."

"That sounds perfect."

"How did you hear about Brownsville? It's kinda off the beaten path."

"I told the clerk at the stagecoach office in San Francisco I wanted to go to the last stop on the line."

"You're a brave woman travelin' so far by yourself. Did you live in the city?"

"A neighborhood on the outskirts. I'm a widow, and if it's all the same to you, Sheriff, I'd rather not talk about it. I'm trying to put all that sadness behind me."

"I'm sorry, and I can sure understand why you'd want to. Are you plannin' to make Brownsville your new home?"

"From what I can see it's appealing. I never was a city girl, but my husband..." she said sadly, letting her voice trail off.

"Don't worry. This is a friendly town and the folks will welcome you. Why don't you stop by the office when you're settled? I'll make us some coffee. I can tell you where things are, and fill you in on some of the local characters. We even have a new place to eat. It opened about a year ago and the food's real tasty."

"Thank you. I'd like that."

"The boardin' house is just down here," he said as they turned a corner. "It's close to Main Street, but far enough away to be quiet."

* * *

As they continued to the white two-story house halfway down the block, Cooper wasn't just taken by the young woman's beauty and manner, he was intrigued. She was wearing a hat, but her copper-colored hair was loose around her shoulders, and her bright green eyes sparkled like the stars in the night sky. Her outfit was fetching, and though he knew little about women's clothing it looked expensive. She claimed she'd never been a city girl, but everything about her suggested just the opposite.

"Here we are," he declared, opening the gate and walking up the short path. "Ruby is a nice lady, but she won't stand for any nonsense."

"I'm happy to hear that," she said as Cooper opened the door. "Like I said, I'm looking for quiet."

"Ruby?" he called, stepping inside. "Are you home?"

"Right here, Sheriff," she replied, appearing from a nearby doorway.

"This is Rose Hamilton, just arrived from San Francisco," Cooper declared. "She's thinkin' about makin' Brownsville her new home."

"Delighted. I'm sure you'll brighten things up around here."

"How kind of you to say so," Violet said with a smile.

"I have the perfect room for you. It's my best. The lady who was there left a week ago. Top of the stairs at the end of the passage and no rooms on either side. It's forty cents a night. Is that acceptable?"

"Yes, that's fine. "

"I'll carry up your bag, then I need to get back to check on those boys."

"I heard all about that," Ruby said, shaking her head as she started up the stairs. "I'm glad you've taken them in hand."

"May I ask what happened, Sheriff?" Violet asked.

"Two young men fightin' in the street over a woman's honor. They're sittin' in a cell stewin' and they'll stay `overnight."

"Here's the room," Ruby announced. "I hope it's to your liking."

"I'll be sayin' goodbye," Cooper said, setting her bag inside the door.

"Stop by the office when you're ready. I'm always around."

"Thank you for everything, Sheriff," she said softly. "You're such a gentleman."

As her green eyes sparkled up at him, Cooper felt it again. The strange sensation moving through his body. But he felt something else as well. The need to watch out for her. He was sensing a vulnerability that belied her confidence and poise.

"My pleasure," he replied, striding back to the stairs.

* * *

"Looks like you've got yourself a fan," Ruby said quietly. "The sheriff's taken with you."

"I think he was just being kindly, but Ruby, he was, uh, not wearing a shirt."

"Please, call me Ruby, and no, he doesn't when it's overly warm. I'm sure you find it shocking, we all did when he arrived, but we barely notice it anymore."

"When I met him I didn't know where to look," Violet giggled.

"The sheriff's a bit of a rogue. He does things his way, but he's the best sheriff this town has ever had, shirt or no shirt!"

"I can't imagine ever getting accustomed to seeing him that way," Violet said, shaking her head, "but it's certainly made my arrival memorable."

"It's not often we have lovely young ladies arrive here by themselves, and when you stepped out of that stagecoach, I'm sure it was a memorable moment for the sheriff as well. Now about the house. I lock the front door at nine-o'clock. If you think you'll be later just tell me. I serve dinner at six o'clock. There is one thing I should mention, though I'm sure it's not necessary with you, but I make it a point to warn all new guests."

"You need to warn me?"

"As I said, I'm sure I don't need to, but the sheriff has his own way of dealing with lawbreakers. He's a fine man, the finest, and he's fair, but he doesn't let anyone sin and walk away unpunished."

"I'm not sure I understand."

"Cooper is the sheriff and he takes his job very seriously. This is his town, and he has his own set of laws and his own justice."

"I don't plan on robbing the bank," Violet joked, "but what do you mean, his own justice?"

"Like what he's done with those two boys. I don't think it's against the law to fight in the street, but it's against *his* law, and he's got those two young men behind bars for the night. And Rose," she said dramatically, lowering her voice, "he's been known to spank a woman."

"You're not serious!"

"I most certainly am. He spanked one of the saloon girls for stealing from a customer."

"I can't believe it."

"But I'm sure it's not something you'll have to worry about. I'll leave you to your unpacking, and if you need anything just let me know."

"Thank you. I know I'll be very happy here."

"You're welcome. It's a pleasure to have you."

As Ruby left, closing the door behind her, Violet took stock of what she'd just heard. She found Cooper's free spirit captivating. They were so much alike. He led his life as he saw fit, just as she did. The sight of his naked chest and muscled arms had made her weak at the knees, and thinking about the saloon girl, a mischievous smile curled her lips.

CHAPTER FIVE

Detective Frank Connelly was seething. Violet Parker had beaten them again. She was the smartest, wiliest, slipperiest swindler, man or woman, he had ever run across.

"She's gone, Frank. She could be anywhere by now," Sergeant Doyle declared. "She gave away almost everything she had. Her neighbors were crying they were so upset she'd left. Everyone loves her."

"She's a criminal, dammit, not an angel. She needs to be found!"

"She's an angel to the people she's helped, and if you ever did manage to catch her and lock her up, you'd have a mob on your hands."

"You mark my words, I *am* gonna catch her. Just a matter of finding out where she's run off to."

"Maybe she gave away her belongings as a smoke screen and she's still here. I wouldn't put it past her."

"I think she's gone. I was getting too close. But why did she visit that wealthy neighborhood before leaving?"

"She must have decided to pull one last job."

"Or maybe that last swindle was a spur of the minute thing. Maybe she wanted to leave from the ritzy part of town."

"Excuse me, Sergeant Doyle," a constable said, knocking on the door and poking his head around.

"Yes, what is it?"

"I think Violet Parker may have—"

"Violet Parker!" Frank exclaimed, jumping to his feet. "Tell me."

"There's a sales clerk from a dress shop at the front desk. She said a woman came into her store claiming to be married to Harold O'Connor, the man who makes O'Connor's Tonic."

"Get to the point, constable!"

"This woman asked the sales clerk to send the bill for the dress she bought to the Palace Hotel because that's where she was staying with her husband. After she left, the sales clerk started to get worried so she went over there and—."

"And there was no Harold O'Connor registered," Frank interjected. "What's the sales clerk's name?"

"Mildred Thomas."

"Show her in."

"Maybe this will be a break," Patrick suggested. "At least we'll know what she's wearing."

"Sir, this is Mrs. Thomas," the constable declared, walking in with the woman following.

"Hello," she said nervously. "I'm so worried. I'm sure I'll lose my job. At the very least I'll have to pay for the missing garments. How could I have been so foolish?"

"Nice to meet you, Mrs. Thomas. I'm Detective Frank Connelly. This is Sergeant Patrick Doyle. You mustn't blame yourself. If it was Violet Parker who came into your shop you're not to blame. She could sweet-talk a gold miner out of his secret map. What did this woman look like?"

"Long reddish-brown hair, bright green eyes, that's what struck me, her eyes. She was a beautiful woman, and so well-spoken. She was dressed in decent clothes but they were badly wrinkled. A white blouse and a grey skirt."

"That's her," Frank said solemnly. "I assume she left in the outfit she bought."

"She did."

"Please describe it to me, then tell me everything that happened."

"It was a brown silk blouse and a dark brown skirt, very expensive."

"Excuse me, Mrs. Thomas," Connelly said, moving from behind his desk. "Sergeant, step outside with me for a moment."

As Frank strode out the door, Patrick followed, then closed it behind them.

"Patrick, find the closest stagecoach depot to this woman's shop, and make sure you get the truth when you question the clerk. Violet's no dummy. She would have told him some cock-and-bull story to keep him quiet."

"I'm on my way," Patrick replied solemnly. "I'll find out whatever he knows."

"Mrs. Thomas, I'm very sorry you were taken in by Violet Parker," Frank said, walking back into his office, "but you've done a great service reporting this. We'll have a much better chance of finding her from the description you just provided."

"I was embarrassed, but my husband insisted."

"He was right, and if you have any trouble with your employer tell him to come and see me. Miss Parker has what the Irish call, the gift of the gab. Now tell me exactly what happened. I'll take a report, and when I catch her you'll have the satisfaction of seeing her punished."

"Do you think you will? Catch her I mean."

"Yes, Mrs. Thomas, I am a very determined man."

* * *

Violet had unpacked, changed her clothes and tidied her hair. Rose Hamilton was a pretty name and it suited her, but she found herself wishing the captivating shirtless sheriff could call her Violet.

Checking her wristwatch, an expensive gift given to her by a dear man who had tragically passed away, she discovered it was almost four-o'clock. There was no fine hotel to enjoy high tea and conveniently forget to pay the bill, but she decided to check out the new eatery the sheriff had mentioned.

Hiding what little money she had in various places, she took what she thought she'd need, including the rent for Ruby, placed it in her black draw string handbag and left the room. As she started down the stairs she could hear Ruby humming. Following the pleasant sound she found her dusting in the parlor, a cozy room with a couch and arm-chairs, and an impressive fireplace.

"Isn't this lovely," Violet remarked as she walked in. "I'm sure this is most welcome on cold winter nights."

"Hello, Rose, yes it is."

"I want to pay for five nights," Violet declared, retrieving two dollars from her bag and handing it to her, "though I'm sure I'll be here longer."

"That's fine. Thank you. You do look smart."

"I gave my best outfits away, all except for one. I couldn't bear the thought of traveling with a trunk, and with my husband passing away I didn't want to keep them anyway."

"What a shame he died so young. Forgive me, I didn't mean to assume..."

"It was tragic, but it isn't something I like to talk about."

"Of course it isn't. Where are you off to?"

"I thought I'd take a wander down Main Street."

"You'll find the folks here very pleasant. Have a nice time."

"Thank you. I'm sure I will."

Leaving the parlor, Violet walked down the hall and out the front door. The air was mild, and the sun was gentle and low in the sky. She let out a happy sigh. Her troubles in San Francisco were behind her, and she was reinventing herself in a sweet little town that was run by a hand-some sheriff. But the image of Detective Connelly unexpectedly float-ed through her mind.

She shivered.

Tall and lanky with a handlebar mustache, he gave her the willies. She'd miss her friends, but she was very pleased to be far away from the city, and most especially from him.

CHAPTER SIX

Cooper whittled. He did his best thinking when he whittled. Mostly he carved animals and gave them to the town's children as a reward for being well behaved. As he sat in his chair on the porch in front of his office, and moved his knife over the wood, he found a cat taking shape. He paused. He couldn't remember ever whittling a cat. Usually it was a dog, a horse or a cow, never a cat, but the branch knew what it wanted to be and there was no arguing with it.

Rose was in the forefront of his mind. She was intriguing, and he couldn't shake the feeling she wasn't quite who she appeared to be. Her clothes and her manner suggested money, but she didn't wear gloves. It was true most of the women in Brownsville didn't either, but Rose was from San Francisco. If she was from money, or married to a wealthy man, gloves would be a habit. He was also curious about her lack of luggage. She had arrived to start a new life, but all she had was a single bag. "Something's not right," he muttered as the cat's face began to take shape. "She either left in a hurry, or she didn't want people knowin' she was leavin' for good. It has to be one or the other."

"Good afternoon, Sheriff."

It was her voice.

Raising his eyes, he saw a vision walking towards him. She was dressed in a pale blue dress, and he immediately liked it better than the brown blouse and skirt she'd been wearing when she'd arrived. It was fresher, prettier, more like her.

"Afternoon, Mrs. Hamilton."

"Please call me Rose."

"I didn't want to presume. Are you settlin' in?"

"I am. It's a lovely room and Ruby is very kind."

"Are you here to collect on that cup of coffee?"

"Or we could have it at that new place you were talking about. I poked my head in. It looked inviting."

"Best I stay in my office," he said, rising to his feet. "Folks will know where to find me if I'm needed."

Ushering her inside, he closed the door behind them, and placed his small branch and knife on his desk.

"I made this just a little bit ago," he said, moving across to a small stove in the corner. "I think you'll like it. I have a special way of brewin'. I even have china cups."

"I'm impressed. How did that come about?"

"I often have folks in for coffee, and one of the ladies decided I should have somethin' decent to serve it in. Have a seat."

"Thank you, Sheriff," she said, settling into a chair.

* * *

To her surprise he walked directly in front of her and perched on the edge of his desk. His bare chest and bulging biceps were alarmingly close, and they were making it difficult to think clearly.

"I reckon you'll be doin' some shoppin'," he began, snatching her attention.

"What makes you say that?"

"You arrived with only one bag."

"I have a special way of packing," she said, tilting her head to the side and holding his gaze, "and that bag holds a great deal more than you might think."

"Is that right?"

"It is, Sheriff."

"Does that mean you've had to pack often? Did you and your husband travel?"

"We did, and he didn't like me bringing more than one suitcase. I'm used to traveling without a lot of baggage."

"Huh. What line of business was he in?"

"Sheriff," she said, rising to her feet and standing eye to eye, "why are you asking me all these questions?"

"I'm curious. It's not often an attractive woman arrives in Brownsville by herself, dressed nice and with nothin' much arrivin' with her. You're a mystery, Rose."

"A good mystery I hope."

"You tell me," he said softly. "I gotta say, it's not normal for a woman to have so little, especially if she's fixin' to start a new life."

"Sheriff," she began slowly, a slight frown creasing her brow, "is it true you spanked a saloon girl for stealing?"

The question had come out of the blue, and she could see she'd caught him off guard.

"Sure is."

"Is that something you do often?"

"As it's needed."

"I can't imagine you'd ever do that to me. That would be ungentlemanly."

An almost indiscernible curl at the edges of his lips was her only warning, but she caught it too late. He suddenly grabbed her wrist, pulled her forward, landed two quick swats, and just as abruptly released her.

"Sheriff!" she exclaimed indignantly, hating the hot red flush crossing her face. "I cannot believe you did that!"

"I hear that a lot!"

"But—you had no right!"

"Ever hear about an ounce of prevention?"

"My goodness!"

"Just so we're clear, do somethin' wrong I give a warnin'. If it happens again, it's over my knee for a good wallopin', third time the dress comes up. Fourth, the drawers come down. That's only happened once. The woman wanted to call my bluff. You remind me of her. She had real mischief in her as well."

Violet was too flustered to come up with a retort, but she wasn't upset. On the contrary, she'd succeeded. He was no longer interrogating her.

"Mrs. Hamilton—"

"Rose!" she said vehemently. "Please, Sheriff, call me Rose."

"Rose, here's your first warnin'."

"For what? I haven't done anything."

"Your sure did. You dared me to spank you in a very connivin' way so I'd stop askin' questions. Next time you try somethin' like that I'll bend you over my leg. If you don't wanna answer that's okay, but you tell me so."

"Fine," she muttered, unnerved he'd seen through her.

"I'd sure like to know why you left San Francisco and brought just that one bag."

"Sheriff, you're the law in this town and I respect that, but I just met you, and I'm not in the habit of telling a stranger all about myself. Thank you for the coffee," she finished briskly, and placing the cup on his desk, she shot him a look, then turned and walked towards the door.

"You'll find Al's Mercantile will have most of what you need."

"Excuse me?" she said, looking over her shoulder.

"Al's Mercantile. He has women's things."

"I'll bear that in mind. Good day, Sheriff."

"Rose, wait! There are two things I need to say before you go."

"Very well," she replied, pivoting on her toes.

"I'm not askin' questions cos I'm bein' nosy, I'm askin' cos it's my job. I need to know who's movin' into my town, and like I said, you're a mystery."

"What's the second thing?"

"I'd like to get to know you better, and not just cos I'm the sheriff."

"If you want to get to know me," she murmured, moving slowly back to him, "I'll need to call you Cooper."

* * *

Her green eyes were mesmerizing, the aroma of her seductive perfume was wafting around him, and he suddenly felt a desperate need to wrap his fingers into her hair, hold it tightly in his fist, and kiss her for endless minutes.

"May I call you Cooper?"

Her voice was like a whispering wind, her face was perilously close to his, her hand was touching his arm...

"Sheriff! Sheriff!"

Jeb's panicked cry rang sharply through the air.

The spell had been broken.

Rose stepped back, and Cooper slid off his desk.

"Don't go anywhere," he said softly, and hurrying across the room he darted through the door that led to the cells.

CHAPTER SEVEN

The moment Cooper was out of sight, Violet moved swiftly from his office and into the street. She was breathless. She'd slipped into her flirtatious routine to gain control of the situation, but when Cooper had fixed her with his dark brown eyes, she'd needed to run away from the unexpected desire flaming through her body.

Such things did not happen to her!

She was the one in control.

She was the one who made a man's head reel, not the other way around. Al's Mercantile was close by, and not wanting Cooper to see her when he came out of his office, she hurried down the street and entered the store.

"Can I help you?"

She quickly scrutinized the man behind the counter. He was older, had very little hair, a large belly and a wide smile. She'd have no trouble winning him over.

"I haven't seen you here before," he continued. "You must be new in town. I'm Alan Walker, but folks just call me Al."

"Lovely to meet you," Violet said warmly. "My name is Rose Hamilton. I just arrived and I'm staying at Ruby Elwood's boarding house."

"Are you stickin' around a while?"

"I'm not sure yet," she said honestly, wondering how long she'd be able to tolerate being around the half-naked sheriff. "I'll just have to see what happens. In the meantime there are a few things I need."

"Take your time. The store isn't goin' anywhere."

"Aren't you funny," she giggled. "Humor is so attractive in a man."

"And you are one charmin' young lady."

She was starting to feel better.

She was back in control.

Al Walker was in the palm of her hand.

"You're too kind. I hate to ask, but I have to be careful with my pennies. Do you have any goods on sale?"

"Why don't you pick out what you need and I'll give you a discount. Just my way of welcomin' you to Brownsville, but don't tell anyone," he added with a wink.

"Mr. Walker. You're so generous. Thank you."

"Please call me Al, and it's my pleasure."

She hadn't brought any toiletries with her. Not only were bottles heavy, she'd needed the room in her bag for clothing. Feeling like herself again, she wandered through the store selecting what she needed.

"I think that's everything," she declared, carrying three small bottles up to the counter.

"That's not very much," Al remarked. "I thought young women nowadays liked all kinds of lotions and potions. You don't need them though. You're lovely just as you are."

"Al, you're embarrassing me."

"Just speakin' the truth. Are you sure that's all you need?"

"For the moment, and I wouldn't want to take advantage of your generosity."

"Don't you worry your pretty head about that. Let's see what we've got here," he said, discounting the items one at a time and placing them in a bag. "There you are, Rose."

"Thank you again for being so kind," she purred, handing him the ninety-five cents he'd charged her. "I really am very grateful."

"Please come back soon."

"Thank you, Al. I most certainly will."

Walking slowly to the door, she peered out the window to see if Cooper was in sight. With no sign of him she stepped outside, and at a fast clip she started down the street towards the boarding house. But she was plagued with a burning question.

Why was he having such a profound affect on her?

Was it simply because he was shirtless?

Telling herself she was just exhausted from the long journey, she turned the corner at the end of the block and walked up to the house. Happy to be there and looking forward to a nap, she stepped inside, but as she neared the staircase, Cooper suddenly appeared from the parlor.

"There you are," he declared, striding towards her. "Been shoppin'?"

"Uh, yes. I didn't bring any, uh, bottles with me," she replied, feeling her face flush. "Why, uh, why are you here?"

"We didn't have a chance to finish our conversation."

"Oh, good, you're back," Ruby declared, bustling down the hall from the kitchen. "I was just making the sheriff some coffee. He'll be joining us for supper tonight. We want to officially welcome you to Brownsville."

"Really? That's so thoughtful."

"Are you all right, dear? You look a little feverish."

"I think I'm a bit tired from my trip, and I must admit I'm frightfully hungry."

"Put your things away, then come back down and chat with the sheriff in the parlor. I'll bring you a snack to tide you over."

But the last thing Violet wanted was to be alone with the sheriff again. Just standing in front of him was making her pulse race, but she was ravenous.

"That's an excellent suggestion, Ruby" Cooper said warmly. "That's just what she needs. Food and some rest."

"You make yourself comfortable, Sheriff, and I'll bring you that coffee and a slice of cake."

"Can't say no to an offer like that! I'll see you in there, Rose."

"Yes, all right. I'll only be a minute," she replied, unable to resist the temptation of something to eat. "Thank you, Ruby. I'm very grateful."

Still unnerved, she gripped the bannister as she started up the stairs. Glad to reach the landing she turned down the hall, and when she entered her room she moved swiftly to the bed and flopped herself down. "I'm just tired," she muttered. "I'm tired and I'm hungry. That's all there is to it."

But she knew better.

Cooper Dalton was having a profound effect on her.

She'd almost had a heart attack when he'd appeared from the parlor.

Closing her eyes she took a deep breath and tried to settle her nerves.

"I don't have to stay in this town. I can always move on, and if things get too difficult that's exactly what I'll do."

CHAPTER EIGHT

Determined not to let the handsome sheriff get to her, Rose brushed her hair, took a deep breath, and left the room. Moving down the stairs she could hear him talking to Ruby, though she couldn't make out what he was saying, but reaching the foyer his voice became clear. She smiled. He was talking about the hot weather. Relieved they weren't discussing her, she moved down the short passage and into the comfortable parlor.

"I've made you a ham sandwich and coffee," Ruby declared, "and there's a small slice of cake for you as well."

"That cake was amazin'," Cooper exclaimed, standing up from the couch as she entered. "I'm sure you'll enjoy it too, Rose. It's about the best I've ever had."

"Sheriff, you always say that!" Ruby said with a smile.

"No-one bakes a cake like you do, Ruby, and that's the truth."

As Violet sat on the chair across from him, she eyed the sandwich hungrily, then picked it up, took a bite, then a second, and washed it down with her coffee.

"My goodness, I knew I was hungry but I didn't realize just how much until this minute," she said earnestly. "Ruby, thank you."

"It's entirely my pleasure. I'll fetch the coffee pot. You'll need a refill in a minute."

"When was the last time you put food in your stomach?" Cooper asked as she continued to devour the snack.

"The places where the stagecoach stopped weren't very appealing. I did have a bread roll last night. It was dry though. I didn't care for it."

"You did all that travelin' and you didn't eat?"

"I didn't think about it," Violet replied honestly. "With the jostling of the carriage my stomach wasn't feeling very well."

"Poor child," Ruby tutted, overhearing Violet's comment as she returned with the coffee pot and filled their mugs. "I'm sure you'll feel better now, and I am sorry but I must get back to my kitchen. Sheriff, I look forward to seeing you in a couple of hours. Just leave everything when you're done, and Rose, be sure to take a nap."

"I will. Thank you again."

"You sure disappeared quick," Cooper remarked after Ruby had left. "When I came back from seeing those boys you were gone, not even a goodbye."

"I didn't know why you'd been called away or how long you'd be. I wanted to pick up the few things I needed, then get back so I could have a lie-down."

"Uh-huh."

"What was so urgent? Was one of those boys in some kind of trouble?"

"A rat was runnin' around. Apparently the older boy is terrified of them. He was so scared he was standin' on the cot shakin' like a leaf."

"I don't blame him. Rats are hideous creatures. Were you able to get it out of there?"

He paused, then took a breath.

"Yep, I got it outta there, but Rose, I reckon I owe you an apology."

"For what?"

"It's my job to learn about the folks that move into this town, but you were uncomfortable. I should've backed off and waited until you'd settled a bit. I didn't mean to upset you."

"I'm just tired, Sheriff."

"Regardless, I'm sorry. I am gonna say one thing though."

"You're right about this cake," she remarked. "It's excellent. What's that flavor?"

"Rose, you're real good at changin' the subject, but I am gonna say what I need to."

Reaching for her coffee mug, Rose used it as an excuse to lower her eyes. He'd cottoned on to her again. Was she being clumsy in her attempts to steer the conversation? Was she really that exhausted?

"It's obvious you left San Francisco in a hurry. If you're tryin' to get away from someone, you'll be safe here. I'll watch out for you, and that's a promise. If you're runnin' from the law, you'll still be safe here. You don't know me, but a few years back I was a bad man."

"You?" she said, staring at him in disbelief. "I find that hard to believe."

"I was a fighter. I was a gambler, and I was a gun-for-hire. I was headed for a wooden box or a square cell, but I met a man who saw some good in me, good I didn't even know I had. That's why I became a sheriff. I wanna help people the way he helped me. There are some folks in this town with a history, not a good history, but they got their second chance."

"Why are you telling me this? Do you think I'm some hardened criminal?" she asked, pretending to be shocked that he might believe such a thing. "Are you suggesting I might need a second chance?"

"I'm just sayin' if you do, or if you're in some kinda trouble, you can count on me. Maybe you're not, maybe you're just a lady who's a bit different and doesn't need a lotta paraphernalia, but if you do need help, I'm your man. There's only one rule. You've gotta come clean, all the way clean. If a fella's been givin' you trouble, I need to know what kinda trouble and everything involved. If you've gotta problem with—"

"Excuse me, Sheriff. The only problem I have is that I need to lie down. I don't know if it's because I've finally eaten, or if the journey is catching up with me, but I really am feeling rather queer. I'm sorry, I need to go," she murmured, rising unsteadily to her feet, "but I do appreciate what you said."

"Can I help you up the stairs?"

"I, uh..."

A wave of giddiness came out of the blue, and just as she thought she was about to fall, he darted forward and caught her arm.

"I'm takin' you up to your bed then gettin' the doc," he said solemnly, sweeping her up.

"No, really," she managed, wondering why her voice sounded so feeble. "I'm fine. I just need some sleep."

"You're seein' the doc," he said firmly as he moved into the hall. "You're about as fine as a rainy day in the middle of winter. Ruby?"

"You called, Sheriff. Oh, my stars!"

"She was passin' out. I'm takin' her up and fetchin' the doc."

"I'll come up and get her into bed while you're gone."

"This is too much fuss," Violet mumbled as he carried her up the stairs.

"Little lady, there's somethin' the matter with you and we're gonna find out what it is. You're probably just tuckered out, but you're in my town and that means you do as I say. You're goin' to bed and seein' the doc."

She surrendered, and it wasn't just because she was feeling too weak to resist. She was lost in the sheriff's strong arms, and the glorious feel of his naked chest against her face.

CHAPTER NINE

Cooper had laid Violet on the bed, but to his dismay her dizzy spell appeared to be getting worse. She was whimpering and mumbling things he couldn't understand. Growing more worried, he'd left her with Ruby and hurried away to fetch the doctor.

Violet couldn't think. Not only was her head foggy, she felt sick to her stomach and she didn't have a stitch of strength. As Ruby undressed her and covered her with blankets, she wanted to protest, but couldn't find the strength, and sank into the mattress and closed her eyes.

"Landsakes, child," Ruby said, sitting on the edge of the bed and moving the hair from her face. "You're as white as a ghost, and you're skin and bone. I sure would like to know what happened to you, but don't worry, I'm not leaving your side until Doc Blake gets here."

"Doc Blake?" Violet managed, lifting from the haze. "What happened to me?"

"You were dizzy and the sheriff brought you up here. He's gone to fetch the doctor."

"Yes, I remember now. I suddenly felt funny, I still feel funny. It was probably the trip. It wasn't very nice."

"Those coaches are dreadful. All that bouncing around! It's no wonder you're not feeling well. Not to worry. I can hear someone coming up the stairs. That will be the doctor."

"Tell the sheriff thank you."

"You can tell him yourself," Ruby assured her as there was a knock on the door. "Come on in."

"How is she?" Cooper asked, walking in with the doctor at his side.

"A little better."

"I'm just a bit worn out from that journey."

"Doc Blake, this is Rose Hamilton," Ruby said, rising to her feet.

"Hello, Rose. It's a pleasure. Now let's take a look at you."

"No, honest, I'm all right."

"The doc's gonna check you out," Cooper said firmly. "Let's go downstairs, Ruby."

"Can I get you anything Doctor Blake? Coffee perhaps?"

"No, but thank you."

"Then we'll see you in the parlor when you're done."

Waiting until they'd left and closed the door, the doctor sat on the edge of the bed and placed his hand on Violet's forehead.

"You are pale," he remarked, "but you have no fever. Tell me what happened."

"I stood up, and then I felt ill and everything started to spin."

"The sheriff tells me you may not have eaten much in the last couple of days," he continued, feeling the glands around her neck. "Is that true?"

"Most of the places the coach stopped at weren't very good, and the ones that were cost too much."

"You sure are thin," he said with a heavy frown. "You didn't get that way in just a day or two. You've gotta tell me how you ended up in such a state."

"There's nothing to tell. It was just a long journey."

"You don't have to worry,. Anything you say won't be repeated to another livin' soul. That's the doctor's oath."

"I'm just tired."

"That's for darn sure. Exhausted more like. The week before you left San Francisco, how much did you eat?"

"Uh, I don't remember. Maybe a bit. I was saving for this trip, and other people needed the money more than me."

"Other people?" he asked softly.

"For their little ones."

"You mean children?"

"Uh-huh. I hated to leave them," she said sadly. "I had no choice, but it's fine, really. I just need a good night's sleep."

"Why did you have no choice?"

"I, uh, I can't talk about that, not to you, not to anyone, and please don't tell the sheriff," she begged, then realizing she should probably tell the doctor the truth, she whimpered, "To be honest, doctor, I uh, I don't feel fine at all."

"You're sufferin' from lack of food and rest. You need to stay in bed for a day or two, and I'll be tellin' Ruby to start feedin' you. I'm also leavin' a tonic. It'll help. A good swallow three times a day. I'll be back to check on you in a couple of days."

"Thank you, Doctor Blake. My bag, it's on the chair. I can pay you."

"You can pay me by doin' what I say. Eat and rest."

She watched him leave the room, and swept up by a long yawn, she closed her eyes and snuggled under the bedcovers. She'd never felt so tired in her life, but she felt safe, and as she drifted away she knew she'd sleep in peace.

There was no fear of the beastly Detective Connelly bursting through her door with his constables blowing their whistles, and Cooper said he'd watch out for her. She hadn't had anyone looking out for her in a very long time, not since her parents had died and she was sent to the orphanage.

Recalling the horrible place made her cringe. She'd escaped and made her way in the world on her wits. But regardless of what he'd said about giving people second chances, she could never tell him the truth about herself. He was a lawman. She couldn't risk it.

Yawning again she surrendered to sleep, and her last thought was how marvelous she had felt being carried by the handsome sheriff, and the feel of his strong arms holding her.

CHAPTER TEN

Joining Ruby and the sheriff in the parlor, Doctor Blake had given them the reassuring news that Rose would recover, and there was nothing seriously wrong.

"But there will be if she doesn't stay in bed for at least a couple of days and get some nourishment," he warned. "I don't know what happened to her, but that young woman has been through a very hard time. She's literally been wastin' away."

"Did she tell you anything about herself?" Cooper asked. "Do you know why she hasn't been eatin' or sleepin'?"

"Now, Sheriff, you know I can't repeat anything she may have said, but she's a special young woman."

"I may have only known her five minutes but I couldn't agree more," Ruby said earnestly. "She's so pleasant and polite."

"She is both of those things, but that's not what I'm talkin' about. I'm sorry I can't say more than that. Just know she's got a generous soul, generous to a fault."

"That doesn't surprise me one bit," Ruby declared. "She strikes me as a very kind young lady. Wouldn't you agree, Sheriff?"

"A kind young lady, yes," he murmured, thinking Rose was carrying a secret.

"She's probably asleep by now. The poor girl was tuckered out," the doctor said solemnly. "I don't know when she had her last meal, and if she eats too much too soon she'll get an upset stomach. Some broth to start, then a small amount of beef and vegetables tonight. See how she does with that. If there are no problems you can increase the portions tomorrow."

"I want to take care of her bill," Cooper said, rising to his feet. "What do I owe you?"

"Thank you, Sheriff," the doctor replied, also getting up, "but I'll tell you what I told her. I don't want any money."

"But you came over here, you should be paid."

"I appreciate the offer, but it was an honor to treat her. I'll be back in a couple of days to see how she's doin."

"Thank you, Doctor," Ruby said gratefully. "I'll make sure she gets what she needs."

"She's worthy of your kindness, Ruby. I'm glad she's here."

As Ruby walked him to the door, Cooper sat back down and tried to make sense of what he'd just heard. The doctor's glowing approval had made a profound impression.

"Who are you Rose Hamilton?" he muttered to himself. "What are you hidin'? Or is it someone you're hidin' from?"

"My goodness, that has my curiosity stirred up," Ruby remarked as she walked back in, "but folk are entitled to their privacy and Rose is no different.. Can I get you more coffee, Sheriff?"

"No, thank you, Ruby. I'd best be gettin' on."

"You're still invited to dinner."

"That's real kind of you, but—"

"I insist. Excuse me for sayin' so, but you're alone too much, Sheriff."

"Not every man is made for marriage, Ruby."

"Every man surely is," she retorted, "you just haven't accepted that fact yet, but you will. When you meet the right woman, you will."

"I'm not sure what to say to that."

"That's because you know I'm right. I'll expect you for the evening meal at six just like we planned, but we'll still have that special supper for Rose when she's feelin' better."

"Yes, ma'am," he agreed with a grin, picking up his hat. "I'll see you then."

She walked him to the door, but as he stepped outside and started down the street, he couldn't ignore the feelings rattling through him. Holding the lovely young woman in his arms and carrying her up the stairs had stirred his heart—and his body. In spite of the repeated attempts by the ladies of the town to get his attention, he'd felt no interest. Why was Rose different? Still deep in thought as he turned the corner, he decided to stop into Al's Mercantile. Rose had been shopping there. Perhaps she'd said something that might give him a clue about her life in the city.

"Sheriff!"

It had been a woman's voice, and he saw Hannah waving at him from across the street. As he waved back she gestured urgently for him to join her. It was late in the day, the street was busy, and dodging the horses and hackneys he jogged over to find out what was so urgent.

"Hannah, what's the problem?"

"No problem, but I heard there's a new woman in town."

"News travels fast."

"I heard she's from San Francisco. Is that true, Sheriff?"

"From what I understand," he said vaguely. "Where did you hear about this?"

"From Mary Jamison. She overheard the woman talking to Al. Mary said she's real pretty. Do you think she's pretty, Sheriff?"

"I can't say I noticed, and why are you askin' me all these questions? I'm a busy man."

"A girl's curious. Mary said the woman went into your office and stayed a while."

"I'll see you later, Hannah. I don't have time to gossip."

"But, Cooper, this isn't gossip."

"Sheriff," he corrected her, looking at her sternly.

"Won't you please come to my house for supper?" she begged, ignoring his reprimand. "Ma and pa would love to have you."

"You know I won't. Be a good girl and go on home."

"Stop talking to me like a child," she said angrily. "I'm seventeen."

"Hannah," he said softly, "you're a very sweet girl, but you've gotta find a nice boy and forget about me."

"You're not much older than I am."

"Maybe not in years, but that's neither here nor there. I like you but not in that way. Now do as I said. Go on home."

"Or what? You'll spank me?"

"Nope, but I'll sure as heck tell your ma to take a wooden spoon to your backside if you keep pesterin' me. Go on now."

"This isn't fair."

"Life often isn't, Hannah, but you've got it better than a lot of other girls your age. You'd best remember that."

As he turned and walked away he heard an exasperated grunt. There was nothing he could do for her, and putting the conversation out of his mind, he hurried back across the street and continued on his way to Al's.

* * *

Detective Frank Connelly was beginning to worry. His sergeant was taking an inordinate amount of time returning from the stagecoach depot. He was almost ready to send a constable to find him when there was a knock on his door and the man walked in. Frank jumped to his feet.

"So? What did you find out?" he asked urgently, "and what took so long?"

"The sales clerk on duty around this afternoon had already left. I had to hunt him down at his house."

"What'd he have to say?"

"I described Violet and he claimed he'd had a busy day and couldn't remember her, but when I threatened to bring him in for further questioning, it jogged his memory."

"And? Don't keep me in suspense!"

"Not a lot of detail. He said he couldn't recall where she was headed, and he made a good point. He said she could have left the coach at any stop along the way and boarded another coach or a train to who-knows-where."

"Yeah, I know, but this is a lead. Looks like you're going on a trip."

"Me? The wife won't like that."

"Too bad. Take that same coach tomorrow. I know these drivers switch routes but maybe you'll get lucky and it'll be the same guy. Get off at every stop and talk to people. Find out if anyone remembers her. Did she continue on, did she leave to go somewhere else? Follow the trail!"

"Okay, boss."

"You'll find her, and when you do, bring her back and don't let her out of your sight for a second."

CHAPTER ELEVEN

It had been a very pleasant evening at Ruby Elwood's boarding house. There were four lodgers at the dinner table, and the conversation had been easy and affable.

But throughout the meal Cooper couldn't stop thinking about Rose lying in her bed just up the stairs. Ruby had taken her a tray, and when she'd collected it, she'd found the plates empty and the girl asleep. Cooper had experienced a wave of relief, and after enjoying a mug of coffee and a slice of cake, he felt okay about leaving.

"It's a strange thing, Sheriff," Ruby said as they were saying goodnight at the door. "I took a liking to that girl the minute I saw her, and it seems you did too."

"I reckon I did. There's just somethin' about her."

"Her eyes for a start." Ruby said softly. "They're like emeralds how they sparkle, and there's a lot going on behind them, you mark my words."

"No question about it. Al said the same thing. I stopped in after I left here this afternoon. I wanted to see if she'd told him anything about herself."

"Did she?"

"Nope, just that she was watchin' her pennies. He said he gave her a discount."

"Al gave her a discount?" Ruby declared. "That's not like him."

"He was just as taken with her as we are. There's somethin' special about her, but I just can't put my finger on it. I'd best be goin'. If you don't mind I'd like to stop by and see how she is tomorrow."

"Of course I don't mind, and I'm sure she'd be pleased if you did."

"Much obliged, and thanks for the delicious meal."

"I'm glad you enjoyed it, Sheriff."

As he walked down the short path and turned towards Main Street, he glanced up at the clear night sky. The moon was coming full, the air was cool, and the stars were twinkling brighter than he thought he'd ever seen them.

His mind began to wander, and his conversation with Ruby Elwood began to replay itself in his head.

Rose was a delight and extremely pretty, yet he was sure she was carrying a heavy burden. In a city the size of San Francisco, such a beauty would have no trouble finding a gentleman. Was that the problem? Was she the victim of an unhappy breakup?

"I need to stop thinkin' so much," he muttered as he turned the block. "I'll find out soon enough."

He could hear the sound of the saloon, and deciding to stop in and make sure everyone was behaving themselves, he crossed the street and pushed through the swinging doors. It was busy, but in the evening it usually was. The girls were gathered around the piano, there were some poker games in progress, and the usual crowd at the bar.

"Hey, Sheriff," one of the girls called. "Come and join us for a sing-along."

"Thanks, Josie, but I need to get back to the jailhouse before I head home," he answered, ambling across to her. "Any trouble?"

"Nope, hardly ever is, and that's down to you."

"Just doin' my job."

"When are you gonna find a nice girl and settle down, Sheriff?"

"I'm already married to this shiny badge right here on my chest."

"Except when you're not wearin' that shirt," she giggled. "I'm always glad when it's hot, and today was no different. Too bad it had to cool off tonight."

"You're a sassy woman, Josie."

"Maybe I am, but does that piece of tin keep you warm in bed?"

"Nope, but it keeps you safe."

"You think you can't have both?"

"I think it'd be a might difficult."

"Nah...that's just an excuse. You know what I think, Sheriff?" she said, lowering her voice as if sharing a secret. "I think maybe you're scared, but that's okay, most men are," she said, then broke into a hearty laugh. "You'll brave up one of these days."

"I'm thinkin' this conversation is over," he chuckled. "You have a good evenin.'"

"You too."

As he ambled back through the room and nodded his regards to the many customers, Josie's words echoed through his head. The girls were always jibing him about making one of them an honest woman, and though he'd never given their jokes a second thought, Josie had been partially right.

The idea of sharing his life with a woman was daunting. He'd seen how men ran home to their wives, worried they'd get in trouble if they were late. He couldn't imagine being under a woman's thumb, and whenever he'd been called out to calm fighting couples, he'd promised himself he'd never wed.

His father had passed away when he was just a boy, and though his mother had done her best, after her husband died she'd rarely smiled. She'd tried to hide it, but her grief had been frightening to witness. He couldn't imagine loving someone as deeply as she had loved his father.

Reaching his office and unlocking the door, he ambled in, lit the lantern on his desk, and carried it through to the cells.

"Come on, Jeb, I'm puttin' you in a separate cell so you'll have a cot for the night."

"Thanks, Sheriff."

"See any more rats?"

"No, thank the good Lord," Charlie replied, "and I hope it doesn't come back."

"I'll leave the lantern. The light will help. Will you boys think twice about fightin' out in the street again?"

"I won't I swear," Charlie said earnestly. "I don't ever wanna be locked up again."

"What about you, Jeb?"

"I, uh..."

"Jeb?"

"Ma says I shouldn't make a promise I can't keep, and if Charlie or anyone else says bad things about Molly I've gotta stand up for her, I just gotta. Wouldn't you, Sheriff, if you were sweet on a girl?"

Cooper felt an unexpected surge of energy pulse through his body. He knew if someone insulted Rose he'd be hard-pressed not to throw a punch.

"Find other ways, Jeb. Knuckles and guns aren't the answer."

"What would you do?"

"Yeah, Sheriff, what would you do?" Charlie parroted. "My pa says a man's gotta fight back or he ain't a man."

"It's tough sometimes, no question," Cooper remarked as he put Jeb in the adjacent cell. "Every situation is different. Talk about that tonight and tell me what you come up with in the mornin'. Looks like you enjoyed the food from the saloon," he added, picking up the empty bowls. "I'll be seein' you in the mornin', then you'll be free to take off."

"Bye, Sheriff," they said, almost in unison.

"Bye, fellas."

But Cooper wasn't about to leave them alone, not with a burning lantern and Charlie being terrified of rats. He'd spent many nights on the couch against the wall. That's why he'd brought it in, so he could stay overnight if he needed to. They wouldn't know he was there, and they'd spend a scary night in their cots. The lesson would be learned, but he'd need to have a word with Zeke Johnson about Charlie. The man's advice was having the wrong kind of impact.

Quietly removing his boots and hat, he stretched out and sighed wearily. It had been a long day, and as he closed his eyes the image of Rose floated through his mind.

She was in trouble.

He was determined to find out what that trouble was.

CHAPTER TWELVE

Patrick Doyle's evening had not been quite so pleasant. When he'd returned home and told his wife, Erin, that he'd be leaving the following afternoon to track down Violet Parker, she had fixed him with her most fierce scowl.

"Chase the girl if Connelly says you must, but you'd better not bring her back!"

"Erin, please! What else can I do? It's my job."

"You listen to me! Violet Parker has done more for abandoned wives and their children than any single person should. She deserves a medal, not prison!"

"She's also a liar and a thief."

"She's a saint! I know for a fact she went without food to buy for the children. Would you do that? If you don't fill that fat belly of yours every night you're not fit to be around."

"She swindled herself a dress near Nob Hill. The sales clerk might lose her job."

"Violet would only have done something like that with good reason. I'll bet she needed to change her clothes because you and your boys were hot on her heels."

"Well, yeah, but—"

"But nothing! Patrick Doyle, I swear to you, if you bring her back you'll have hell to pay, and not just from me!"

"What do you want me to do? I'm a policeman. I have to enforce the law."

"Like when your pals drink too much and get into brawls? Or what about Johnny Clark trying to steal that jacket? You gave him a reprimand and sent him on his way."

"That's different. Violet Parker never stops."

"Have you ever met her? Ever talked to her?"

"Only in the alley when she was pretending to be a victim of herself. Imagine that? A victim of herself. I should have recognized that hair of hers. I don't know why I didn't."

"Sounds like you're upset because she outsmarted you."

"I am, darn it! Frank had a fit, and George Griffin is cleaning toilets for the next month."

"I don't like that detective. I never have. He has evil in his eyes."

"Now, Erin, he's a senior officer, and he's also my boss!"

"I don't care if he's the Mayor, he has the devil in him, you mark my words."

"This is all beside the point. He's sending me out to track down Violet Parker and bring her back to face justice."

"Justice? Justice is about as fair as an armless man trying to fight a fella with a gun."

"Don't you understand? It doesn't matter if her reasons were noble. She broke the law, and she broke it many times. She needs to pay the price. That's how it works."

"You do what you want, Patrick Doyle, but it seems to me you'd be wise to follow her example."

"What example is that, pray tell."

"For once in your life, do the right thing!"

"Hey, I married you, didn't I?" he said, attempting to kiss her and put an end to the argument.

"That was twenty years ago. Remember what it felt like, and try to be as smart as you were back then."

Later, sitting at the large oak dining table, surrounded by his five children, laughing and acting up as they ate their supper, Erin's warning replayed itself in his head.

If you bring her back you'll have hell to pay, and not just from me!

He was stuck.

He couldn't disobey orders, but he sure couldn't go against his wife when she was so adamant. She volunteered with several local charities. She knew Violet and had always sung her praises. He had to get on the stagecoach and pick up the trail, but after that he had no idea what he was going to do.

* * *

"What did I tell you?"

"I'm sure I don't know what you mean."

"I said if you deliberately changed the subject to get outta answerin' a question I'd bend you over my knee. Isn't that what you just did?"

"I, uh..."

The shirtless sheriff grabbed her wrist, and as he placed his foot on a chair and pulled her over his thigh she yelled a protest, but when his hand began landing hot smacks across her backside, it took her breath away. He was scolding her as he spanked, but as abruptly as the hot slaps had begun they came to a stop. He pulled her up, and gripping her upper arms he fixed her with narrowed eyes. In spite of the humiliation burning across her face, she was consumed with a scorching fever. She wanted him to hold her, to kiss her, to take her body and soul.

Bolting upright, Violet stared around the room.

She didn't know where she was.

In a flash she remembered.

"Brownsville," she panted. "I'm in Brownsville. Heavens, what was that?"

The curtains were open, and the early morning sun was streaming through her window. It was a new day in a new town, and she knew why she'd had the startling dream. She wanted Cooper to spank her. Bringing the covers up to her chin, she thought back to the events the afternoon before. She remembered fainting in the parlor, and Cooper's strong arms as he carried her up the stairs. Resting her head against his chest had been heavenly, but when he'd laid her gently on the bed, she'd been unable to keep her eyes open.

"I'll rest for just a bit longer and I'll be back to normal," she murmured, but as her eyes closed, she felt the weariness deep in her bones.

* * *

A gentle knock on his office door woke Cooper from a deep sleep. Worried something terrible had happened he staggered to the door and opened it, only to find Rose wearing just her chemise and drawers.

"Whatta you doin'? Folks will see you! Get in here."

"I don't care. I can't stand it another minute. I must confess my sins. I need you to spank me then make love to me. I'm a wily willful woman, and I need a strong man like you to be happy."

"I need you too," he crooned, taking her hand and leading her across the room. "I reckon those boys will be sound asleep, but the sound of my hand slappin' your backside might wake 'em up. I'm gonna use a little stick. It'll sting just as good—if not more."

It didn't seem to bother her that he was completely naked, or that his cock was standing at attention. Fetching the twig from his desk drawer, he took her to the sofa, laid her over his knee, and pulled down her drawers. Her bottom was even lovelier than he'd imagined, and he began softly caressing the plump curves.

"Start tellin' me your sins, and I'll punish you as I see fit."

He couldn't understand her mumbling confession, but he danced his little stick regardless, and when she threw her hands behind her and looked over her shoulder with pleading eyes, he tossed it aside and pulled her into his arms.

"Come here, darlin," he murmured lovingly, *"sit on my cock while I suck your beautiful breasts, then I'll ride you up the mountain and we'll take off and fly together."*

He woke with a start.

Someone really was knocking.

He had no idea of the time, and moving unsteadily across his office, he turned the key and opened the door. It was George, Charlie's brother.

"Are you okay, Sheriff?"

"Yeah, fine, what's up?"

"It's gone past eight."

"It has?"

"Pa sent me. One of the hands saw a group of strangers near the back fields, but they took off when he started ridin' toward 'em. Pa's worried they might be rustlers. Asked if maybe you could come out and have a look see."

"Tell him I'll be there before noon."

"Thanks, Sheriff. How's that little brother of mine?"

"Learnin' his lesson, but I'm runnin' late. It's a good thing you came by."

"Okay. See ya later."

Closing the door, Cooper ran his fingers through his hair. His cock was as hard as a steel rod, and being in the office he couldn't take care of the urgent need. Pulling on his boots, he walked uncomfortably around to the back of the building and ducked into the barn. R
ose Hamilton was crawling under his skin, and he knew there wasn't a darn thing he could do about it.

CHAPTER THIRTEEN

Though Cooper had told Ruby he'd stop by after lunch to check on Rose, he needed to ride out and see if there was any sign of the rustlers. and he wouldn't be back until mid-afternoon. But he was grateful. He was eager to see the girl who had unexpectedly stirred his heart, and he had a legitimate excuse to drop by early.

As he released Charlie and Jeb, they told him how they could handle confrontations without using their fists. Though he had difficulty paying attention, Cooper nodded his head and gave them his approval. But when he walked them outside, he discovered the weather had changed. Running home to grab a shirt, he hurried to Ruby's front door, lightly knocked and stepped inside.

"Sheriff, thank goodness you're here," she exclaimed, walking quickly up to greet him. .

"What's wrong?"

"It's Rose. She's refusing to follow Doc Blake's orders. She's up there right now getting dressed."

"Leave this to me."

Moving swiftly past her and trotting up the stairs, he marched down the short hall to her room.

"Rose? It's the sheriff," he declared, knocking loudly. "I need to speak with you."

Only a moment passed before he saw the handle move down, and as the door cracked open, Rose peeked at him through the narrow space.

"Sheriff?"

Staring into her mesmerizing green eyes, he felt the odd scintillating sensation ripple through his body. It wasn't easy, but doing his best to ignore it, he summoned a stern expression.

"Ruby tells me you're fixin' to get dressed."

"I am. I'm going—"

"Back to bed!" he said sternly, cutting her off. "That's where you're goin' young lady, and right now!"

"That's silly. I was a little tired when I first woke up, but now I feel just fine."

"Are you gonna do as you're told?"

"If I don't will you spank me?"

Her comment started him, but he quickly recovered and leaned forward.

"I just might if you don't do as I say."

"I, uh..."

"I don't see you movin'. Get on back to that bed."

"I, uh..."

"I heard that the first time. Let me make this real clear. I'm gonna count to five then I'm comin' in, and if you're not under those covers I'll put you over my knee, pull down your drawers, and spank you hard! If you're well enough to get up, you're well enough to feel my hot hand on your bare backside."

The threat had spilled out of his lips before the thought had barely crossed his mind, but watching the bright red blush cross her face he was glad he'd made it.

"I'm already h-half-dressed," she stammered. "I'm not sure I—"

"Then you'd better get undressed right quick. One—"

"Heavens!"

She'd gasped the word as she quickly disappeared from view, but he continued counting, and pushing open the door when he reached the number five, he found her scrambling between the sheets.

"Just as well," he said sternly, moving a chair from against the wall and taking it to her bedside. "You wanna tell me what you were thinkin'?"

"Like I said, I feel fine."

"Doc Blake says two days, and that's what it's gonna be...and more if he thinks you need it."

"I didn't know it was against the law for someone to get dressed and go for a walk."

"What if you passed out in the middle of the street?"

"It wouldn't be the first time," she mumbled under her breath.

"I didn't hear you. What did you say?"

"Nothing, nothing," she replied hastily. "Has anyone told you you're a bully?"

"There's a difference between bein' a bully and takin' charge, and in this case, young lady, takin' charge is needed."

"You don't care that I just called you a bully?"

"Nope, cos you didn't mean it. Deep down you know I'm only bein' this way cos it's for your own good, and you are gonna get those smacks on your butt just as soon as you're feelin' better."

* * *

As Violet felt the unfortunate blush return to her cheeks, butterflies suddenly burst to life in her stomach, and she couldn't find her voice.

"You don't wanna know why?"

She did want to know, desperately, but all she could manage was a nod.

"Like I said, it's fine if you don't wanna tell me somethin', but then you say, I don't wanna talk about that. Remember?"

"Uh..."

"You muttered somethin' under your breath, and when I asked you about it you accused me of bein' a bully. You did that to distract me so you wouldn't have to answer."

Guilty," she mumbled, lowering her eyes.

"It's a habit, and I'm guessin' it's one that works on most everyone, but you'd best remember it won't with me. Are we clear?"

"Yes, Sheriff, and I'm going to talk about something else now."

"Go right ahead."

"It's not fair."

"What's that?"

"Being cooped up in here when I could be outside enjoying my—enjoying this lovely day."

"Enjoyin' your what?"

"My new town," she said quickly, "but I don't know how long I'll be here so I don't want to call it that yet."

"That's not what I heard."

"What do you mean?"

"I heard, *when I could be outside enjoyin' my freedom.*"

"If that's what you heard, then there's something wrong with your ears." He studied her for a moment, then rising to his feet he started across the room.

"Are you leaving?"

"Nope, just closin' the door."

"You're closing the door and it's just the two of us in here?"

"Are you worried, Rose?"

"Um, no, but Ruby might not like it."

"I'm doin' it for you."

"For me?"

"Yep," he replied ambling back to her. "We need to have a chat, and you'll feel better if we have privacy."

She was sure he'd closed the door because he was going to pull the covers, roll her over and swat her backside. Tthough she was relieved, she couldn't deny her relief was tinged with disappointment.

"There's something wrong with me," she said with a heavy sigh, wondering why she wanted the sheriff's hot hand slapping her backside.

"Of course there is. You're tuckered out and starvin', or are you talkin' about somethin' else?"

"Um, something else, but it's too personal to tell you."

"And that's just fine, Rose. You see how easy that was?"

"Uh-huh."

"Now you need to listen. Can you do that for me?"

"Uh-huh."

"I don't know what you're runnin' from, but I'm pretty sure that's why you're here," he said solemnly. "I think you're in some kinda trouble and I wanna help, but the only way I can is if you're willin' to trust me."

CHAPTER FOURTEEN

His declaration had been earnest and sincere, and a hot lump suddenly sprang up at the back of her throat. To have someone on her side, someone strong like him, would be a dream come true, but how could she confess all the things she'd done. He was the sheriff.

"If you've done somethin' you think you can't tell me cos I'm a lawman, like I said before, there are people in this town who thought that too," he said, as if reading her mind. "They were wanted some for real bad things, but I let them stay and gave them a second chance. I told you, someone did that for me once, and now I'm doin' it for others. Brownsville is far enough off the beaten track folks can feel okay about startin' over, and they know their secrets are safe with me—unless they mess up, then they're in real big trouble."

"So, um, if I told you certain things, you wouldn't ever tell anyone?"

"If that's how you want it, not a soul."

"I don't understand. Isn't your job to catch bad people?"

"I think I just explained that, and I may not know you real well, but I don't think you're bad, Rose. I'm bein' straight with you, but if you're not ready to trust me, that's okay."

A single droplet spilled from her left eye and slipped down her cheek. Though she'd been trying to keep her emotions in check, a rogue tear had escaped.

"Rose, please let me help you."

"I want to," she sniffled, "but I'm scared"

"Of course you are, but I won't betray you. We'll find a way through whatever it is together."

"We will? Even if there are other lawmen after me? I'm not saying there are, I'm just saying—if."

"We will, I promise. Did you kill someone, Rose?"

"Kill someone? Heavens above! No! I could never kill someone. I've wanted to, one person in particular, but I couldn't possibly."

"Accidents happen, there's self-defense, certain situations—"

"I haven't, I swear it," she said vehemently, "and I haven't physically hurt anyone—um, that's not strictly true. I did once."

"Are you gonna let me help you?"

"You have to let me call you Cooper."

"Is that the deal?"

"That's the deal."

"All right, Rose, you can call me Cooper."

"I know this might not be proper," she mumbled as the flood gates opened and the tears sprang from her eyes, "but do you think you could give me a hug?"

"Of course," he said softly, and sitting on the edge of the bed, he took her into his arms. "You're not alone anymore. I'm here now. I'm gonna take care of things."

The words washed over her like a warm spring shower. It was too good to be true. Surely it was just a beautiful dream, but as he stroked her hair and repeated his promise, she knew it was real.

* * *

He wasn't sure how long he held her, but Cooper had never been filled with such a stirring need to protect someone. Regardless of what she'd done, or who she'd wronged, he was determined to make things right. When her sobs began to subside and she slowly pulled back, he placed his hand under her chin and tilted up her head. Their eyes met, and there was nothing in the world that could stop his kiss. As he leaned in and softly brushed her lips with his, a flame of hot desire fired through his body. Her arms lifted and circled his neck, his fingers found their way into her hair, and their mouths glided together.

As they breathlessly broke apart, he gazed down at her, and filled with an unfamiliar aching need, he suddenly understood what it meant to want a woman. To want her body and soul.

"Rose Hamilton, you are a treasure."

"Cooper," she whispered, "it's Violet. Violet Parker."

* * *

Sitting in front of Detective Connelly's desk, Sergeant Doyle was even more worried than he had been as he'd tossed and turned through the night. That morning his wife had pecked him on the cheek and wished him safe travels, but her silence about the reason for his journey was louder than anything she could have said. Violet was to be left wherever he might find her, assuming he was able to track her down.

"Patrick!" Frank declared as he marched into his office. "Are you ready to leave?"

"Yep, but it's a different coach driver."

"Damnation. Never mind. You'll find the same people at the stops. What about that clerk? Was he there this morning?"

"No sign of him."

"Leave me his address. I'll pay him a visit myself. Here's a pen and paper, and add the directions."

"It's not hard to find," Patrick said as he scribbled the information. "It's a nice little house in a quiet neighborhood."

"Now listen up," Frank said gravely. "You must remember that girl is as slippery as an eel. If you find the town she's in, and she gets wind there's a lawman looking for her, she'll vanish like a puff of smoke. You can't let anyone know who you are. Be careful how you ask around. I know she's only been gone a short time, but that girl makes friends easy. People like her, they instinctively want to cover for her. You can't let that happen."

"Right," Patrick lied, thinking that might be the answer. If he *wasn't* careful she'd disappear again, and he could honestly say he'd had no luck.

"What's goin' on, Patrick?" Connelly asked, his eyes narrowing. "You don't seem too happy about this."

"It's my wife. She doesn't like it when I'm away."

"Then find that green-eyed witch and get her back here."

"Right," Patrick repeated, and rising to his feet he picked up his bag and started out the door.

"One more thing," Frank called after him.

"Yeah?"

"Wife or no wife, I don't care how long it takes, don't come back without her."

* * *

Frank watched his sergeant walk solemnly out the door, then opening his top drawer he pulled out a package of cigarette papers and a tin of tobacco. Laying the thin tissue on his desk, he expertly filled it and rolled it tightly closed. Smoking helped him relax. It also helped him to think.

As much as he trusted Patrick Doyle, he was worried the sergeant would let Violet Parker slip away. It was possible she had won him over during their short interlude in the alley.

"That girl's a witch," he grunted. "She casts a spell on everyone who crosses her path."

Lighting up his cigarette and taking a long drag, he blew out the smoke and frowned. He'd wanted to go after her himself, but his Captain didn't care about a woman who was a petty thief and swindler. As far as he was concerned, if she was gone, so much the better. But Frank wanted her back, and come what may, he was going to make it happen.

CHAPTER FIFTEEN

As much as Cooper wanted to peel back the bedcovers, slowly remove Violet's nightdress and devour her body, he had to release her and sit back in his chair. There could be no more than the kiss. She had to fully recover, but even if she wasn't sick it wouldn't be right. Their attraction may be as blazing hot as the sun in the middle of summer, but they'd just met, and there was Ruby to consider. Doing his best to ignore his raging erection, he held her for just a moment longer, then slowly let his arms fall away.

"It's nice to meet you, Violet Parker."

"You too, Cooper Dalton. Um, I'm feeling a bit funny."

"You know what? I am too," he said with a grin as he sat back.

"Why am I suddenly tired again?"

"You just took a risk and let out a whole lotta relief. That would tire you even if you were well, which you're not."

"There's so much more I have to tell you," she murmured, a frown crinkling her forehead. "So much..."

"Take it one step at a time. Right now you get some rest. You'll be stuck in this bed for the next little while and we'll have plenty of time to talk about things."

"Cooper, there's something important you need to know before you leave. There's a man after me. He's a beast. I don't think he'll be able to track me down, but if anyone new arrives in town and asks about me, please don't tell them I'm here."

"I'll make sure of it. Who is this fella?"

"Detective Frank Connelly. I did break the law. I'm sorry, I did, but it wasn't for me. It was at first, but—"

"I figured as much, and that's enough for now," he said, cutting her off. "You need to get some rest, and I've got a feelin' once you start tellin' your story it'll take a while."

"He can't find me," she said urgently. "If he does, you won't be able to stop him dragging me away from here."

"Don't you worry about that! No-one's gonna be draggin' you anywhere," he said firmly. "I'm always at the depot when the stagecoach rolls in so I'll know if any strangers show up. What does this fella look like?"

"Tall and lanky, but he's got a pot belly and a big mustache."

"He'll be easy to spot," Cooper declared, rising to his feet. "You do as you're told and rest now. I have to ride out and see about some possible rustlers. I'll stop in if I don't get back too late."

"Cooper?"

"Yeah, Violet?"

"Thank you—thank you for everything. You have no idea..." she murmured, her voice trailing off as a fresh wave of emotion swept through her heart.

"Hey, it's okay," he said softly, sitting on the edge of the bed and taking her hand. "Like I said, you're not alone anymore."

"It's just so hard to believe."

"Believe it. The Good Lord saw fit to have us meet up, and we may just be gettin' to know each other, but there's a feelin' between us, somethin' special. I'm not gonna let that slip away. You understand what I'm sayin'?"

"Yes, I do. It's like magic."

"I don't know what you've been through, but I know it's left you wrung out. Now it's time for you to take a deep breath and recover. You don't need to fret. Those days are over. You relax, get some sleep, and I'll see you later today or tomorrow mornin'."

As she let out a heavy sigh, Cooper leaned forward, kissed her forehead, then slowly walked across to the door, but paused to shoot her a wink before disappearing into the hall.

* * *

Violet was tired and longed to fall back asleep, but there was an urgent need between her legs. Slipping her fingers inside her drawers. she sought out her small sensitive nub. Urgently rubbing, she imagined Cooper completely naked as he peeled off her clothes, then laying her on the bed, he stretched out next to her and wrapped her up in his strong, muscled arms.

Her orgasm was building.

She pictured him sucking her nipples, but the image suddenly changed. She was over his knee, and he was landing hot slaps on her bare bottom. As the powerful climax abruptly seized her, she stifled her cries as the convulsions shuddered through her body. Moments later, completely drained, she imagined she was resting her head in the crook of his shoulder, and drifted back to sleep.

* * *

Cooper found Ruby in her kitchen chopping vegetables.

"How is she? Will she stay in bed?" she asked, pausing to look up at him expectantly.

"She will. We had a long chat."

"I was starting to get worried, but I figured you had things under control."

"She won't be givin' you any more trouble."

"That poor girl can give me as much trouble as she wants. There's something about her...I can't put my finger on it, but I hope she stays. I want to know her better."

"I feel the same," he remarked with a sigh. "But I must be goin'. I'll see you later."

"Bye, Sheriff, and I'm really happy you two have hit it off."

She had a twinkle in her eye, and not knowing how to respond he turned and hurried away.

Stepping outside and walking to the end of the block, he breathed in the fresh air. His head was swimming. His attraction to Violet was almost overwhelming. Willing his cock to go back to sleep, he turned the corner and started down Main Street.

Everything was calm, but that was normal.

Calm and normal was what he needed.

Deciding to stop at Al's Mercantile to alert him there may be unwanted strangers asking questions, he was about to cross the street when he heard Charlie calling. Looking towards his office, he spied the young man waving as he jogged towards him.

"Sheriff, I've been waitin' for you."

"Shouldn't you be back at your ranch? What's the problem?"

"I had a long talk with pa when I got home, and, uh, the thing is, Sheriff, I wanna be a lawman. Can I be your deputy? I figured you might need one since Jerry left."

"It's not quite so easy, Charlie. I can't just put a badge on your shirt. There's a lot to learn."

"I'm sure there is, but how do I start? My pa has given me his blessin'. He and ma both. They said they'd be real proud."

"What brought this on?"

"I wanna be the guy that locks people up, not the one bein' locked up."

"I reckon that's as good a reason as any," Cooper chuckled. "But you need to learn how to be a peacemaker, not a fighter. Do you think you can do that?"

"Sure I can. You just need to show me how."

"You're a strong boy, Charlie. Bein' a lawman would suit you. If you can control your temper and do what I say, you should be just fine. Are you busy right now?"

"No. Can I do somethin' for you?"

"I have to ride out and see if there are any rustlers in the area. While I'm gone, keep your eyes and ears open and write down anything I should know about. But remember, you're not a deputy yet, and you can't be bossin' people around!"

"Yes, sir, Sheriff. Oh, man, I'm so excited. Wait'll pa hears this."

"You can also sweep the place and get the dust off my desk and the table. Around one-o'clock go out back and clean up my horse's corral. You know River, he's an easy-goin' fella. You can give him some hay while you're there."

"Sure will. Thanks again. Can I put Hazel in there with him? She's saddled and tied up at the hitchin' post outside your office."

"No problem. Here's the key to the office. Don't lose it! If you leave, be sure and lock up and put it under the red rock out back."

"Okay, Sheriff. I won't let you down."

CHAPTER SIXTEEN

As Cooper watched Charlie jog down the street, he shook his head and put his hands on his hips. The morning had been full of surprises. With a satisfied grin he walked into Al's Mercantile.

"Hey, Sheriff. Did you just get some good news?"

"Yeah, I reckon I did. Charlie Johnson wants to be my deputy."

"That's one for the books! That boy could've gone either way. What can I get you, Sheriff?"

"I need to talk to you about Rose Hamilton."

"What a sweet girl she is. I hope she stays a while."

"Yep, me too. Thing is, she's got a bad guy chasin' her down."

"I'm sorry to hear that, but I figured somethin' was up. A pretty girl like that doesn't travel all this way by herself with no good reason."

"If anyone asks, tell them you haven't seen a woman fittin' her description, then let me know who was doin' the askin'."

"Be happy to."

"And, uh..."

"Yeah, Sheriff?"

"She's under the weather. I was thinkin' maybe I'd get her a present to cheer her up, but I'm not used to buyin' gifts for ladies. Any suggestions?"

"A nice locket, or maybe a scarf."

"A scarf sounds right."

"We've got quite a selection."

"Have you got a green one?"

"Sure," Al said eagerly, gesturing for Cooper to follow him. "It will match those eyes of hers?"

"That's what I'm thinkin'."

"You've got four to pick from."

"Dang, I don't have a clue."

"This young lady might be able to help. Hey, Hannah, come on over here. The sheriff is wantin' to buy a scarf for—"

"A sick friend," Cooper said hastily, not wanting Hannah to get involved. "But I've made up my mind. That one, it's shiny."

"You picked the costliest. It even comes with a box. I'll be right back."

"Who's sick?" Hannah asked. "Anyone I know?"

"Nope," he said briskly. "What are you doin' in here?"

"Came to get some blister cream and bandages for my mother. She got new shoes and they're bothering her."

"All set, Sheriff," Al called from the cash register.

"Excuse me, Hannah."

Moving away, Cooper was grateful she didn't follow him. Paying for the gift and hurriedly leaving the store, he headed home so he could deal with his engorged cock. It wasn't far, and he was soon in the privacy of his bedroom lying on the bed urgently stroking his swollen member.

He could still taste her lips and feel the fullness of her breasts pressed against his chest. As his climax began to build, he imagined her bent over his lap, her naked backside turning a delightful shade of pink under the hot slaps of his hand. It was enough to push him over the edge. As the spasms rocketed through his loins, his cock jerked in his hand, spurting his essence across his fingers...

"Violet, what have you done to me?" he groaned, still trying to catch his breath.

But he'd never been so elated, and he allowed himself a couple of minutes to relish the heady feeling. Finally slipping off the bed and cleaning himself up, he started back to his office, but a sudden thought occurred to him.

The saloon girls!

Not all of them were trustworthy, but Josie was. He'd stop in and ask her to keep her eyes open for a tall, mustached stranger. If the man chasing Violet did show up, he was likely to stop at the saloon for a drink and the company of the pretty ladies.

* * *

As Patrick Doyle was climbing into the stagecoach, perplexed and distressed by Frank Connelly's parting orders not to return without Violet, the detective was knocking on the door of a modest home in a decent neighborhood. It was owned by Calvin Montgomery, the clerk from the stagecoach office.

He was a decent man, happily married with three daughters, and he had never been in trouble with the law. The unexpected visit from the police sergeant the day before had left him shaken. When he opened the door to a tall, grim man with a ridiculous mustache, and dark eyes under an angry scowl, Calvin felt a bolt of fear.

"Are you the clerk from the stagecoach office near Nob Hill?"

"I am," Calvin replied, hoping he didn't appear as nervous as he felt.

"Detective Connelly," Frank declared, flashing his badge, then pushing past, he walked inside the house and looked around.

"Uh,I spoke to someone yesterday," Calvin declared. "His name was Sergeant Doyle, I believe."

"Calvin, this is going to go one of two ways," Frank said gravely, pivoting on his toes to face him. "You're going to tell me the truth or I'm going to hurt you."

"Hurt me, Detective Connelly?" Calvin asked, trying to summon his courage. "I don't understand. Police officer's don't walk into people's homes and threaten them."

"I do, and I'm warning you! Don't play dumb! A young woman, dark red hair! You sold her a fare yesterday around this time, but you told my sergeant you barely remember her. That was a lie! She's not a female people forget! Especially not a middle-aged married man like you. The truth! Or do you want your wife to come home and find you on the floor with blood on your face?"

Calvin had never been so scared and conflicted in his life.

Not only did he believe he'd suffer great bodily harm if he didn't give the man the information he wanted, he suspected the despicable detective was the reason the young lady had been running away.

"Honey, what's—oh, we have company."

Calvin felt his blood run cold, and turning around he stared at his wife. Her smile was quickly fading. She'd realized the tall man standing in her living room was an unpleasant fellow, very unpleasant indeed.

"Maybe I should ask *her* these questions," Frank snarled, striding across the room and gripping her arm. "I'm sure you come home and tell her everything. She'll be more than happy to provide me with the information I'm looking for, won't you, Mrs. Montgomery?"

"Ow, let me go. You're hurting me."

"Calvin! Three seconds to start talking or I'll punch her right in her pretty little nose, and that's just for starters!"

"Okay, okay, let her go," Calvin begged. "Please, she hasn't done anything."

"I'll let her go when you start blabbing," Frank growled, tightening his grip. "I'm going to start counting. One—

"She didn't give me her name," Calvin shouted. "She said if I didn't know I wouldn't have to lie."

"What color were her eyes?"

"Green, bright green."

"Which stop was she getting off at? So help me if you don't tell me the truth I'll break your wife's arm after I smash her nose in."

"Brownsville, Brownsville," Calvin exclaimed frantically. "The last stop on the line."

"See, that wasn't so difficult, was it?" Frank sneered, shoving the terrified woman towards her husband. "Next time a sergeant comes knocking on your door, tell him the goddamned truth."

"Yes, yes, I will," Calvin promised, wrapping his arms around his shaking wife.

* * *

Frank could feel their frightened eyes follow him as he walked to the front door, and stepping outside, an evil smirk crossed his face.

Brownsville.

He'd never heard of the place, but that's where he was headed.

He couldn't shake the feeling his sergeant wasn't up to the task.

Dealing with his Captain had been easier than he'd thought. Frank had told him there had been a sudden death in his family and he needed a few days off. Though his boss had eyed him suspiciously, he'd agreed. What Frank would say when he got back with the girl in tow he wasn't sure, but he didn't care. He'd think of something. He always did.

CHAPTER SEVENTEEN

Stirring from sleep the following morning, Cooper saw no sunlight through the curtains. Slipping from his bed and padding across the room, he moved them apart looked up at the grey clouds looming overhead. Letting out a yawn, he began to ready himself for the day.

He'd spent longer than he'd intended in his search for the suspected rustlers the afternoon before, and though he'd found an abandoned campground, there had been no sign of the men who had used it. When he'd returned dirty and tired, he'd been surprised to find Charlie still in his office. The young man's enthusiasm was impressive, and as he dressed, Cooper had little doubt his wanna-be deputy would be outside the office door waiting for him to arrive.

But foremost on his mind was Violet.

He'd returned too late to visit and couldn't wait to see her.

He wanted to sit with her, hold her hand, and softly kiss her sweet lips. Pulling on his shirt and buttoning up a jacket, he stuffed the thin box containing the scarf against his ribs. It would be safe if it started to rain, but as he walked out his front door he was met with a swirling gust of cold wind. Thinking they were in for more than just a few drops of rain, he strode to the end of the block and turned into Main Street.

It was ominously quiet.

A shiver rippled through him.

He paused.

It hadn't been from the chill in the air.

Danger was lurking.

His senses on alert he continued on, and as he neared his office he spotted Charlie leaning against the door trying to stay out of the cold.

"Mornin', Sheriff," the young man said as Cooper approached. "Lookin' like it's gonna be a nasty day."

"Mornin, Charlie. Yep. I reckon we're in for a storm," he replied, unlocking the door and stepping into his office. "Did you check on River?"

"Sure did. Hazel is with him, but she sure was edgy ridin' here. My pa says she's storm wary."

"Mare's can be that way," Cooper replied, "and Charlie, besides the weather, I'm feelin' like there's somethin' brewin'."

"Like what, Sheriff?"

"Not a clue, but I'm sensin' trouble'. It's kinda like sniffin' the wind and gettin' a whiff of a scent that isn't quite there yet."

"You just gave me the willies."

"It's good. Keeps you on your toes," Cooper said solemnly, then pausing he added, "Charlie, listen up. There might be an unwelcome stranger comin' into town. Tall fella with a big mustache. His name's Frank Connelly. He's a detective from San Francisco. If he tries to talk to you act dumb, don't answer any questions, then come and find me. But make sure he doesn't follow you."

"What's this about, Sheriff?"

"I can't tell you that right now. Just do as I say."

"You can count on me."

"I'm goin' on my rounds then over to Mrs. Elwood's Boardin' house," Cooper continued as he opened his top desk drawer. "You need to study this. It's a book outlinin' the duties of a deputy along with some basics about crime and punishment. You've got five days to learn it, then I'll test you."

"This is great, Sheriff. Thanks."

"One more thing. Whatever you hear in this office, whatever I tell you, or whatever anyone tells me or you, it's private!" he said sternly. "You don't repeat one word of it to anyone. Not your brothers, not your pa, not your sweetheart, not anyone. You'll be fired right quick if you do."

"Yes, sir, Sheriff. I won't. I swear."

"If it starts stormin' put the horses in the barn and give 'em plenty to eat. I'll see you in a bit."

"Thanks, Sheriff. I'm real happy to be here."

"I'm glad you're takin' the right path. Your pa has a nice spread, but if you'd rather be doin' somethin' besides ranchin' this is a good life. I'll be back in a bit."

Normally Cooper would take his time as he wandered past the shops. He'd peer in the windows making sure everything was as it should be, but he was in a hurry, and only paused momentarily to look inside. He was soon walking through the small gate at the boarding house, and when he stepped inside, Ruby greeted him with a wide smile.

"Come in, Sheriff. You'll be so pleased. Rose has never looked better. Between you and me, I don't think she's been well since she arrived."

"I agree."

"Can I get you some coffee?"

"That sounds good. Thanks. I haven't had any this mornin'."

"You go on up. I'll be there shortly."

Taking the stairs two at a time, he strode down the short hall and knocked on Violet's door.

"Come on in."

As he entered and looked across at her, he let out a happy breath. Ruby was right. There had been no color in Violet's cheeks, but now they were rosy pink, and wearing a pale green robe, with her long copper hair spilling around her shoulders, she looked lovelier than ever.

"You seem a whole lot better," he exclaimed as he walked across the room and stood beside the bed.

"Thank you. I feel amazing. It's going to be very hard to sit in this bed all day."

"But you will, right?"

"Yes, I will. Can you stay?"

"For a bit," he replied, then unbuttoning his jacket, he withdrew the white box. "I, uh, this is for you."

"For me? What is it?"

"I thought it might cheer you up. I hope you like it."

"Cooper! What a wonderful surprise!"

Pulling off the short coat, he placed it around the back of the chair, then sat down and watched her lift out the scarf.

"Oh, my goodness, it's just beautiful. Thank you so much."

"It reminded me of your eyes," he said softly, then feeling embarrassed, he removed his hat and ran his fingers through his hair. "I'm not much good at stuff like this."

"Stuff like what?"

"Givin' gifts and such."

"I'd say you're very good," she exclaimed. "Can I give you a thank you hug?"

"You betcha!"

As he leaned across the bed and put his arms around her shoulders, she placed the scarf around the back of his neck, and he suddenly found himself being pulled towards her.

"Whatta you doin'?"

"Trying to steal a kiss."

Abruptly her lips were pressed against his, the scarf fell loose, and he was engulfing her in his arms. Their passion ignited, but a soft knock on the door sent him scrambling back to his chair.

"I have your coffee, Sheriff," Ruby declared, entering the room carrying a tray. "I figured you didn't have any breakfast, so I've brought you up some porridge with molasses."

"It's so good," Violet said rolling her eyes, hoping she didn't look as disheveled as she felt. "You're a wonderful cook, Ruby. I haven't had food like this in, gosh, I don't know how long. Maybe never."

"We know," Cooper remarked, raising his eyebrows, "and those days are over. Thank you, this looks delicious."

"I have things to do so I'll leave you to chat. If you wouldn't mind bringing the tray back to the kitchen I'd be much obliged."

"Of course," Cooper replied, "and thanks again."

As Ruby left, closing the door behind her, Violet began to giggle. It was contagious, and Cooper began chuckling along with her.

"I feel like a kid doin' something wrong and almost gettin' caught!" he declared.

"That was so funny. You looked so flustered."

"I felt flustered! I still do!"

"Cooper, can I ask you something?"

"You know you can."

"Did you mean it yesterday when you said you were going to spank me?"

Staring at her flushed face, he had an inkling she wasn't asking out of fear, she was asking because she wanted him to.

"I did, and I will, just as soon as you're out of that bed," he promised, "and you were right, this porridge is real tasty."

"If that woman lived in San Francisco she'd be making a fortune as someone's private cook, or working in a nice restaurant."

"Speakin' of San Francisco," he said, lowering his voice and looking at her solemnly, "are you up to talkin'?"

"I'd like that. I'd like that a lot."

"Good. You can start by tellin' me why that detective is chasin' you."

CHAPTER EIGHTEEN

Letting out a heavy sigh, Violet lowered her eyes, then raised them again and stared directly at him.

"It's a long story, Cooper. Are you sure you want to hear it now?"

"I'm sure, and don't leave anything out. How long has he been after you?"

"Ages," she said with a deep frown, "but I need to tell you other stuff first. From the time I was about six I was in an orphanage. It was a horrible place except for one lady. She used to sneak us cookies at night, and fetch extra blankets when it was cold. Then one day she told us she had to leave. She didn't say why, but we all knew it was because she was being too nice and had been told she had to go. I was about twelve when I finally ran away, but I promised myself I was going to do what she did. Find a way to make the lives of other children like me better. That's why the detective is after me."

"Are you sayin' you've been by yourself since you were twelve-years-old? How did you survive?"

"It was hard at first, so I'd pretend to be someone I wasn't just for fun. I found out I could do it really well. That's how I began to make money. I'd find a well-dressed lady, and tell her that my mother had sent me to the store, but I'd lost my change and I'd be in terrible trouble. Then I'd beg her to help me. It always worked. Getting money to buy food for the children in my neighborhood became my reason for living. I still want to help, I just don't know how I can from here."

"And Detective Connelly found out what you were doin.'"

"About two years ago he picked me up off the street and hustled me to the station. He said he could prove I was a thief and a swindler, but I managed to get away. My friends took turns hiding me for a while, and put out a rumor that I'd moved to another part of town. Then he caught up with me a couple of months ago, but I managed to escape again. I knew I had to leave. I did one last thing on my way to the stage-coach and it went wrong. The police had me cornered, but I managed to fool them."

"Why did you risk doing something at the last minute?"

"I'd given almost all my money to this woman who's little boy suddenly got awfully sick, and I needed something for my travels. Do you hate me now you know what I've done?"

"I could never hate you," he said softly, "and I think you're amazin'. I'm not sure what to do about it, or if there's anything that should be done, but if that detective shows up, he won't learn you're in this town from me."

"I feel bad that I'm so happy here, when my friends are still in such an awful way. What will they do without me?"

"You can't save the world," he said gravely. "It's a funny thing, though. I became a sheriff because of what a man did for me, and you became a good samaritan because of what a woman did for you."

"I wouldn't call myself a good samaritan."

"You were to those you helped," he remarked, then placing the tray on the floor next to his chair, he walked across to the door and turned the key.

"Cooper, what are you doing?"

"I need to lie down and hold you," he murmured, returning to sit on the bed and pull off his boots. "I doubt Ruby will be back, but I don't wanna take the chance."

As he climbed on the bed and brought Violet into his arms, a surge of joy surged through her heart, and nestling against his chest, there was nowhere in the world she wanted to be.

* * *

The stagecoach was about three hours outside of Brownsville, and Patrick Doyle was finally at peace. The journey had been boring and uncomfortable, but it had given him time to think.

Being a sergeant in the San Francisco Police Department was a fine job, but it was still just a job. Erin and his children were his life. If he had to choose between them and the force there was no contest. He was almost ashamed that he'd not realized it from the start.

He'd been married to the fiery Irish girl for twenty-five years, and he absolutely adored her. He also trusted her. If she said Violet Parker should be given a medal, he wasn't about to haul the young woman back to the city in handcuffs.

He knew exactly what he had to do.

Absolutely nothing.

He'd enjoy a couple of days relaxing, then go home and tell Connelly he hadn't found Violet or any information about her. If by chance he saw her, he'd look the other way.

He wasn't worried about being kicked out of the police department. He had an outstanding reputation, and he'd known the Captain for many years. But regardless, Erin and his family came first.

* * *

Perched on a hillside a short distance from Brownsville with a chilly wind whipping around him, Frank Connelly was studying the town. Brutus, his sturdy steed, loved to gallop, and Frank had barely stopped during the journey. He figured he'd beaten the stagecoach by several hours, but now hungry and tired, both he and his horse needed food and rest.

But he had to steer clear of the main road through town.

There was no telling where Violet would be.

If she spotted him before he spotted her, she'd vanish in the wind.

He'd passed several ranches, and he could see several more scattered below. If he showed his badge he could probably talk his way into one of them, then he could slip into town during the late evening hours and get the lay of the land. He also needed to learn about the sheriff. Some of the smaller towns had lawmen who were eager to cooperate with the big city police, but others were territorial.

The skies were darkening. There was a storm developing. He had to find accommodation, and quick. Scanning the farmhouses below, he decided the modest homes would probably need the money, but the larger ranch houses would have more space.

Having no desire to be in a cramped hovel with half-a-dozen kids underfoot, and wanting Brutus to have plenty of decent hay, Frank decided on a sprawling ranch house a short distance away.

Mounting up and riding down the hill, he felt the first drops of rain, and as he approached the impressive rambling home, it started to sprinkle. Before he'd even slipped from the saddle the front door opened, and a well-dressed, solidly built man stepped out on the wide verandah.

"Mornin'. You need somethin'? You lost?"

"Good morning. My apologies for intruding," Frank said politely. "I'm Detective Frank Connelly. I'm here from San Francisco on official business."

"Is that so? Zeke's my name. Zeke Johnson. You'd better put your horse away and come inside. It's about to bucket down."

"I'm obliged."

"The barn's over there. You'll find hay and a space for him. He's a fine lookin' animal."

"Thanks."

"Just come on in when you get back. I'll have some coffee ready. Looks like you could use some, then you can tell me what this is all about."

CHAPTER NINETEEN

Cooper hadn't meant for it to happen.

Violet had been resting against his chest, then she'd raised her head and kissed him.

A warm, simple, glorious kiss.

Barely a moment later, she was no longer under the blankets, but next to him with her robe off and his hands inside her chemise kneading her luscious breasts. She'd pulled the thin garment over her head, and there she was, her beautiful mounds completely naked with their cherry tips waiting to be devoured. As he lowered his head and began drawing them into his mouth, she lifted her chest, moaning softly and mumbling his name. Hastily pulling off his shirt and somehow scrambling out of his trousers, he'd groaned as he felt his skin against hers, and only when she started to remove her drawers did he hesitate.

"What is it?" she whispered, staring at him with confusion in her eyes. "Don't you want me?"

"Like I've never wanted anythin' in my life," he said huskily, "but we've just met, we're in a boardin' house, there are so many reasons not to do this."

"I don't care about any of them, and neither does he," she murmured, wrapping her fingers around his engorged cock.

That was all it took.

The train had left the station and it could not be stopped.

Moving his hand to her soft pussy fur, he slipped his fingers into her velvet folds.

"You're so wet. Damn...you're so wet."

"Take me, please, Cooper, take me."

Rolling on top of her, he gently pushed his hardness into her warm, sweet sex. Her mewled utterances of pleasure flamed his need, and he began to thrust with slow, strong strokes. To his great relief the bed made no sound, and as his cock consumed her pussy, he pressed his lips against hers to muffle her cries of joy. He wanted to carry his kiss across her naked body, taste her womanhood, then flip her over and spank her beautiful backside, but such delights would have to wait for another time. Though they had lost themselves in their fervent passion, they were still in Ruby's respectable boarding house and had to end their passionate coupling quickly.

But Violet had never been so swept away.

His arms had her wrapped up in their engulfing hold, and his lips were devouring hers. Lying under his powerfully muscled body was sheer bliss. She never wanted their lovemaking to end, but her orgasm suddenly seized her. Spasm after sizzling spasm shuddered through her body, finally waning and leaving her tingling and breathless.

She was still floating when he abruptly pulled out and spewed his cream across her belly, then collapsed next to her, bringing her with him. Everything fell quiet, until a thunderous roar rolled over their heads and broke the spell.

"I wish we could stay here like this all day," she sighed, then added. "Maybe you could pretend to leave then sneak back in."

"You, Violet Parker, have a very devious mind."

"It kept me alive."

"Yeah, I reckon it did."

As the rain started splattering against the window, Cooper reluctantly slipped from the bed, dressed quickly, then fetched a kerchief from his jacket pocket and gently wiped her stomach.

"You'd best put your, uh, underthings back on. I need to unlock that door."

"Don't you like my naked body?"

"Nope, I *love* your naked body, and I should arrest you for layin' there temptin' me again."

"Or you could surrender to that temptation."

"I already did, and I'm not pushin' my luck. Put your nightie back on," he ordered, then grinning, he added. "It's a crime for me to say that."

Giggling at his comment, she put her bedclothes back on as he walked across to the door. Waiting until she was ready and propped up against the pillows, he turned the key, then ambled back to the chair and sat down.

"You suddenly look very serious," she remarked. "Is something wrong?"

"I hope you don't think I was takin' advantage just now."

"I started it," she said softly, "and I hope you don't think I'm a loose woman. It's just that my life taught me to grab happiness without thinking. I'm not sorry. Are you?"

"Sorry? The only thing I'm sorry about is that we didn't have more time and we weren't at my house."

"That would be wonderful. Do you live far?"

"Just across Main Street and around a corner. I need to live nearby in case of trouble."

"It's comforting to know you're so close. I missed you yesterday."

"I missed you too."

"Did you find any rustlers?"

"Nope, and I'm not goin' out to look again in this weather."

A gentle knock on the door made them share a guilty glance, and a moment later Ruby entered carrying a coffee pot.

"I thought you might need a top up," she said sweetly. "How was your porridge, Sheriff?"

"Delicious. Thank you."

"Can I get you some more?"

"I need to get back to my office. It's days like these I get paperwork done."

"And I'd best get back to my chores. You look the picture of health, Rose, but you must get more meat on your bones, and you probably need a bit more rest."

"I'm not allowed out of this bed until tomorrow, so I don't think getting more rest will be a problem."

"Ruby, I can bring that to the kitchen when I go," Cooper offered as she picked up his tray. "I'll be leaving shortly."

"It's fine. I'm going down, might as well take it."

"Cooper, I wish you didn't have to leave," Violet said softly as Ruby left the room. "Will you come back later?"

"Of course I will," he replied, then drinking down his fresh coffee, he stood up and kissed her on the cheek. "You take it easy."

"Listen to that," she exclaimed as a roll of thunder boomed overhead. "You'll get drenched."

Moving across to the window, he stared out at the torrential downpour. It was holding hands with a fierce wind.

"You know what, you're right. I reckon I'll stay until it lightens up a bit. We can chat some more."

"Can we talk about you?" she said earnestly. "About your family, and how you ended up in Brownsville?"

"I'm happy to tell you all that, but some other time. I want to talk about the future instead of the past."

CHAPTER TWENTY

As a frown crossed Violet's brow, Cooper sat down in his chair, then leaned forward and reached for her hand.

"The future?" she repeated with a frown. "I've never thought about the future...except a couple of days ahead," she replied quietly. "Surviving is like that. Though when I decided to come to Brownsville I was hoping to find a peaceful life here."

"If you could wave a magic wand and make your dreams come true, what would they be?"

"That's easy. I'd be settled. I'd go to sleep without worry, and not wake up scared about what the day might bring. I'd have my own children and I'd be giving them a full, happy life. The kind of life every child deserves, and I'd be helping all those poor little ones in those awful places."

He could hear the emotion in her voice, and it broke his heart to think about what she might have suffered through.

"I reckon you've got a good chance of havin' that dream come true."

"Please may I have a hug?"

"Always," he murmured, leaning across the bed and taking her in his arms.

"Listen," she said softly. "The rain...it isn't pouring...that hug was magic."

"Maybe it was," he remarked, "though it means this is a good time for me to go. But I'll be back, you can count on it."

"Cooper, is this really happening, this, uh, this thing between us? It's so—what's the word? Unexpected."

"I'm as surprised as you are, but it sure is, at least as far as I'm concerned," he said, pulling on his jacket, "and I'll be seein' you real soon."

"Okay. Bye, Cooper."

"Bye, darlin'."

Picking up the mug and heading out, he trotted down the stairs feeling both euphoric and confounded. Violet had swept into town and utterly stolen his heart. He'd never experienced anything like it, and still feeling slightly overwhelmed, he ambled into the kitchen.

"Much obliged for the porridge and coffee, Ruby. Here's your mug."

"Thank you, just put it on that counter. You know, Sheriff," she began hesitantly, "when I first met my dear departed husband, I knew the minute I laid eyes on him that he was the man for me."

"Is that right?"

"He felt it too, and it was only a month later we were wed. We stayed happy together for almost twenty-six years. Why the Good Lord chose to take him so young I'll never know, and I miss him every day."

"Why are you tellin' me this?"

"You know why, Sheriff," she replied, looking at him with a twinkle in her eye. "The question is, are you as brave as the folks around here think you are?"

"Uh...what?"

"Chew on it for a while. Will I be seeing you later?"

"Sure will."

"Doctor Blake will be here around two o'clock to check on our patient."

"Thanks, I'll bear that in mind. Bye for now."

"Bye, Sheriff."

Shaking his head, Cooper walked down the hall and out the front door. It was still raining, but it was light, and as he strode down the block, Josie's words flashed through his head.

I think maybe you're scared, but that's okay, most men are, but you'll brave up one day.

Cooper grinned.

Maybe the saloon girl was right, but he didn't feel scared, and the daunting doubts he'd always felt were giving way to joy. He'd never dreamed he'd be so drawn to a woman, certainly not in the space of such a short time, but he remembered the unfamiliar sensation that had rippled through him when he'd first laid eyes on the copper-haired beauty standing by the stagecoach.

But there was one lurking question.

Violet was obviously experienced between the sheets.

She'd had no hesitation about wrapping her hand around his hard shaft, she'd kissed him without reservation, and there had been no resistance when he'd thrust inside her.

Had she been with many men, or was there someone special in her past?

He'd thought about asking her, but their moment had been too special to spoil with such questions. He was curious more than concerned, and he hoped she knew he wouldn't sit in judgment if she chose to tell him.

* * *

Deliriously happy and sitting in her bed, Violet was moving her fingers across the soft, silky scarf. She'd thought it would take a while to meet a nice man who would be interested in her, but not only had she found him, he was a whole lot more than a nice man.

He was handsome and rugged, warm and kind, and he'd made love to her with gusto, but he'd also been tender and sensitive. He was a dream come true, she cared for him deeply, and she felt as if she'd known him for a very long time. It was obvious he was a man of the world, and she was sure he'd understand when she told him the details of her past. But it was nerve-racking to think about that particular conversation.

"I must tell him the first chance I get," she murmured. "I've had secrets my whole life, but now I don't want them anymore, not a single one!"

CHAPTER TWENTY-ONE

Zeke Johnson was a smart man. His ranch wasn't just the biggest in Brownsville, it was the largest ranch in the county. Whenever he was asked what had made him so successful he always gave the same answer. Numbers.

Numbers liked him. Numbers made sense to him, and his ability to calculate numbers with speed most men found astonishing, had seen him amass land and wealth.

But God had seen fit to gift him with another talent.

His ability to listen carefully and give people what they wanted.

Some people didn't even realize what they truly yearned for until Zeke gave it to them, then they'd feel deeply indebted. But Zeke usually knew the favor he would ask in return would be worth more than the gift he'd given.

He had been blessed with four sons, and to a degree each had inherited their father's cleverness, but his youngest, Charlie, was the smartest. He was also the most difficult. When Charlie took a liking to something, he approached it with no-holds-barred enthusiasm, but when asked to do something he found boring, he'd either flatly refuse or grumble through every moment. Much to Zeke's disappointment that was how Charlie felt about ranching, and if Charlie wasn't going to be a rancher, what would he do?

But once again, Charlie validated Zeke's belief his son would rise to great heights. After being locked up overnight for fighting, he'd come home and made a proclamation.

"Pa, I'd rather be the one lockin' people up, than bein' the one locked up. I wanna be a sheriff."

Zeke had almost fallen on his knees to thank God.

Charlie had finally found his path.

Then he wanted to thank him a second time for his son's irrefutable logic.

When Charlie had asked how he could convince the sheriff to take him on, Zeke had told him to repeat what he'd just said.

Now, as if by fate, or perhaps God's hand, a stranger had ridden up to his front door and introduced himself as a detective from San Francisco.

Immediately Zeke had seen many roads unfold for his son's future.

Charlie's brilliant brain would make him an outstanding detective or an excellent lawyer. Perhaps success even beyond that. Zeke knew a man who had risen from sheriff to become a State Senator. There was no telling how far his sharp-witted son could go, and Zeke believed, if he played his cards right, Detective Connelly would help to pave the way.

"So you see, Mr. Johnson," Frank concluded, after a long-winded description of Violet's many crimes, "apprehending this murderous young woman is of the utmost importance. Beneath her beauty and poise lies a black heart. At the station she's known as Violet the Viper."

"Dreadful business, dreadful," Zeke said gravely, rising from his wingback leather chair. "Would you care for a whiskey? It's a little early in the day, but I think better sippin' on a drink."

"I sure would. It was a long ride."

"After we talk you'll join my wife and I and our sons for lunch."

"I don't want to be any trouble."

"Not at all," Zeke said affably as he splashed the liquor into cut glass tumblers. "Here you are, detective. Let me see if I've got this straight. This young woman, Violet Parker, has been stealin' from the good folks in finer areas of the city, and murdered an older gentleman after milkin' him out of his money."

"That's the long and short of it."

Frank was pleased with himself. Though he'd exaggerated Violet's activities, blaming the death of the man she claimed she was going to marry had added drama to the story.

"And you need to move real quiet so she doesn't get wind of you," Zeke continued. "If she does, you say she'll vanish like a ghost. I do understand that part of it, but there is one thing I'm havin' trouble with."

"What's that, Mr. Johnson?"

"That you believe our sheriff may have been influenced by this woman. I know Cooper Dalton, and he's not a man to be influenced by anyone, let alone a wily female."

"You don't know her. She's not just wily, she has seductive green eyes, long reddish-brown hair, and a figure any man would be hard-pressed to walk away from. I have no doubt she's already made it a point to befriend your sheriff and fill his head with stories of the nasty San Francisco police, and how she's been falsely accused of crimes she didn't commit."

"But if she is here, she's just arrived. She's had no time to do such a thing."

"Honestly, Mr. Johnson," Frank said, leaning forward and lowering his voice, "sometimes I've wondered if she's a witch. She always knew when we were about to pounce. I can easily imagine her seducing your well-meaning sheriff the moment she arrived just in case I was able to track her down."

"Well, I admit the sheriff does tend to give people a second chance if he feels they deserve it. Your caution may be warranted. I have a suggestion," Zeke said thoughtfully. "My youngest son has just started workin' at the sheriff's office, and he's a bright boy, very bright. I'll go into town and visit him. He'll know if this woman has arrived and if the sheriff has met her. I'll talk with the townsfolk as well. People won't have any trouble sharin' their gossip with me. I'm well-respected in these parts."

"Mr. Johnson, I can't thank you enough."

"Weather's kinda bad, but the storm will probably pass overnight. First thing tomorrow I'll go into town and see what's what. In the meantime you're welcome to stay. I've got plenty of room, and the missus will be happy to chat with someone from the city."

"Won't your son be home tonight?"

"When this boy gets excited, there's no pullin' him away. He mentioned he might not be back when he left early this mornin'. He'd rather sleep on an old sofa in the sheriff's office than come home to his comfortable bed. That's just the kinda dedication he has, and I couldn't be prouder."

"This is excellent news," Frank said gratefully. "I'm expecting my sergeant to arrive today. I don't want to show myself, but I must make sure he's arrived safely and find out where he's staying. I need to know where the stagecoach depot is, and watch it without being observed."

"Don't bother yourself," Zeke exclaimed. "I'll send George. He's my oldest. He's good friends with the man who runs the place. Tim Hardy. Just describe your sergeant's appearance and George will hang around and get the information."

"This is too much to ask, Mr. Johnson."

"It's my duty, detective. If Violet Parker is in Brownsville, I've gotta do what I can to help you catch her. George will find out where your man is stayin', and when I go into town in the mornin' I'm sure I'll find out where this young woman is too."

Zeke watched the detective's face light up like a Christmas tree.

Sometimes life was so easy it was shameful.

CHAPTER TWENTY-TWO

It was mid-afternoon when the stagecoach rolled into Brownsville. Forced to move slowly through the bad weather, it was arriving later than usual. As Cooper approached to meet the tired passengers and scrutinize any strangers, he noticed Charlie's brother George talking to Tim Hardy.

"Hey there, George," Cooper said walking up to shake his hand. "Are you here to check on your little brother?"

"I'll stop in and see him, but no, I came to see Tim."

"Tell your pa I did a scout around for those rustlers and there's nothin' to report."

"Sure will, Sheriff."

The carriage came to a stop, and as the passengers climbed out into a misty rain, Cooper saw only one stranger. A rotund middle-aged man with pink cheeks, red hair poking out from under a cap, and bright blue eyes. Cooper guessed him to be Irish,

"Can I help you? I'm the Sheriff," Cooper said, approaching him with a smile. "Was someone supposed to be meetin' you?"

"Hello, Sheriff. My name's Patrick Doyle, and no-one is supposed to be meeting me."

"Are you here on business, Mr. Doyle?"

"No, no, nothing like that. I just fancied a day or two away from the hustle and bustle of the city."

"San Francisco I assume."

"It's a busy place. I swear it never sleeps, but if I'd known it was going to take me so long to get here I might have chosen someplace else."

"There are towns along the way. Why didn't you stop in one of those?"

"Maybe I should have, but I'm here now, and I'm glad," Patrick declared. "It seems very quiet and calm."

"Yep, it is, and I like to keep it that way."

"I don't suppose there's a hotel."

"Not as such. There's lodgin' at the saloon, but it can get rowdy later at night."

"A boarding house perhaps?"

"I'd recommend the MacTavish's. All men, except for the wife of the proprietor of course, good food, not too expensive."

"Sounds perfect. Don't expect to see much of me, Sheriff. I may just sleep for two days."

"A long way to come to sleep."

"There's sleep, and there's sleep. No noise. That's why I came. Where is this boarding house?"

"Go back the direction the coach came in, and you'll see a turnoff surrounded by trees."

"I remember seeing that. It's not far at all."

"Nope. Just go down a ways and you'll see a red and white house. If you want quiet, that's the place. The church is just up from there."

"Thank you, Sheriff. I'll head over there right now. A cup of tea and a bed is what I need."

Cooper was feeling no threat from him, but his reason for being there wasn't plausible. It was a long journey for just two days, and the small towns along the way would have offered him the same peace and quiet. "Have a nice rest, Mr. Doyle."

"I'm sure I will," Patrick replied, then turned and started towards the edge of the town.

Watching the stranger head off, Cooper guessed the man had another reason for visiting Brownsville. But as long as he didn't cause any problems or hurt any of the townsfolk, he was welcome.

Turning in the opposite direction, Cooper hurried down Main Street hoping to see the doctor before he left Ruby's. Though he arrived too late, Ruby filled him in. Violet could leave her bed the following morning, but she needed to take the tonic until the bottle was empty, eat three meals a day and have early nights.

"This is excellent news," Cooper said happily. "I can't thank you enough for what you've done. You took care of a stranger the way you would a dear friend."

"You know I took a liking to that girl the minute I laid eyes on her. She's got a good heart, I just know it. But why is a young woman like that traveling all this way by herself? It's not right."

"No, it's not, but I've made sure she knows she's among friends, and now I think I'll go up and pay her a visit."

"Feel free. I'm sure she'd love to see you. Stay as long as you want."

Ruby had twinkled up at him as she'd spoken, and feeling slightly embarrassed, Cooper grinned his thanks and hurried up the stairs.

"Violet, it's me," he said as he knocked on the door. "Can I come in?"

"Yes, please do!"

As he walked inside, she looked so happy he strode quickly across to her and wrapped her up in a bear hug.

"I heard," he said as he squeezed her tightly. "You'll be up and about tomorrow."

"I feel as if I've been locked up in this room for a week."

"Just be glad you fainted among people who care about you."

"I am...very," she said gratefully, pulling back and staring at him. "I don't know how I'll be able to repay the kindness I've been shown."

"Do as you're told and get even better!"

"I'm not sure about the first bit, but definitely the second."

"I'd be careful if I were you," he chuckled. "You're already set for two spankin's. You wanna third?"

"Cooper!"

"Just sayin.'"

"Why don't you kiss me instead?"

With his cock already stirring in his trousers, he leaned in, pressed his lips against hers, and moved his hands to her breasts. She mewled softly, then let out a little yelp as he tweaked her nipples.

"There's a whole lot I wanna do to you, Violet Parker," he murmured huskily.

"Lock the door and climb into bed with me."

"We're gonna wait until tomorrow. I'm gonna take you to my house and we'll have privacy and time."

"But I don't want to wait."

"But you will," he whispered in her ear, then moved his lips to her neck. "Darlin', what we did yesterday was—"

"Heavenly, Cooper. Absolutely heavenly."

"Yeah," he growled, gripping her hair and pulling it back to gaze into her eyes, "but I've got a few surprises in store, and makin' you wait is just the beginnin'."

"I feel all weak."

"But this time it's a good weak," he said with a wicked smile. "There's another reason you have to wait. Charlie's waitin'. I need to take him around all the stores and make sure folks know he's workin' for me now."

"I'm sorry you have to go so soon."

"So am I," he said as he released her and sat back in his chair. "Just keep thinkin' about tomorrow. Waitin' can be half the fun."

"I feel as if I'm living a dream. I can't remember when I was this happy. I don't think I ever have been. I had no idea when I stepped off that stagecoach how quickly and how wonderfully my life would change."

"It was just another day for me, then suddenly it wasn't."

"One thing's for sure, I never expected to be greeted by a half-naked sheriff," she declared with a wink. "I didn't know where to look."

"I wasn't half-naked. I just don't wear a shirt on hot days!"

"You were naked from the waist up, that's half-naked."

"I suppose," he said with a grin, then suddenly remembering the red-haired man he added, "Violet, have you ever heard the name Patrick Doyle?"

"Patrick Doyle," she said thoughtfully. "Doyle rings a bell. There's a Mrs. Doyle who works with a charity in my neighborhood. Why do you ask?"

"A stranger arrived in the stage coach today. That's his name. He said he wanted to get away from the noise of the city and have some peace and quiet. He seemed harmless enough, but I thought perhaps he might work for that detective who's after you."

"Could you do me a favor?"

"Name it."

"If Detective Connelly does show up here, please be very careful. He's a mean, sneaky, dangerous man."

"Violet, why don't you tell me what else happened with him?" Cooper said softly. "I know there's more to the story."

"Yes, uh, all right. He tried to, uh, he attacked me, but I shoved my knee between his legs. He mauls all the women he brings in for questioning." Cooper felt a searing heat wash through his body. As far as he was concerned, crimes against women and children were second only to murder.

"He steals from them too, whatever they have on them. He keeps everything in a locked drawer in his desk. I know because that's where he put my money and the bracelet I was wearing. I saw all kinds of stuff in there. No-one ever gets away from him, but I did, and I'm sure that's why he's so determined to find me."

"Don't you worry," Cooper said with a scowl. "If he shows his face here, I know exactly how to deal with him."

"You have to be extremely careful," Violet warned earnestly. "You don't know what he's like."

"You're wrong, darlin', I know exactly what he's like, but he doesn't know a thing about me, and if he does come into town, he's in for a big surprise."

CHAPTER TWENTY-THREE

To Cooper's surprise, when it came time to close for the evening, Charlie asked to stay the night in the office. Cooper agreed, but wanting to learn more about his potential new deputy he invited him back to his house for supper. The women of the town would often gift Cooper casseroles and pies, and earlier in the day Al's wife had brought him a beef stew. As he stirred it on his stove, he could sense Charlie was nervous.

"I'm glad you could join me," Cooper said, hoping to make him more comfortable. "It's nice to have the company."

"Thanks so much for bringin' me here, Sheriff. I feel real honored."

"It's my pleasure. Tell me more about yourself."

"What would like to know?"

"Why do you want to stay in the office? You live in a nice home. Are there problems?"

"It's nothin' like that. I just wanna be outta the house. My brothers want to stay there 'til they get married, but that's not for me. Pa's ranch is great, but ranchin', isn't for me."

As he dished the stew into bowls, Cooper thought about Charlie's earlier comment about wanting to lock people up rather than be locked up. It had been clever, and while it was doubtless true, Cooper now understood the deeper motivation behind Charlie's wish to work for him. Charlie was his own man. He wanted to make his own way in the world.

"Does your pa understand?"

"Sure. He's known for a long time. He doesn't care what I do as long as I'm satisfied doin' it. He has my brothers and they love the job."

"Speakin' of your brothers, I saw George today," Cooper remarked, carrying the bowls to the table and sitting down. "He was at the stagecoach depot."

"Yeah, he stopped by to say hi, but it was strange."

"Strange that he stopped by to see you?"

"No, not that. It was strange for him to go to the depot. Tim doesn't like him there, especially when the coach arrives. There's too much goin' on and he says George gets in the way. They always meet at the livery stable then go to the saloon. This stew is real good, Sheriff. Who made it?"

"Mrs. Walker. She's a good cook. But all the ladies in our town are good cooks. There are a lotta lucky men here, but gettin' back to your brother, if that's the case, why did George go there? He must have had a reason."

"He said he was helpin' pa."

"Pickin' up a package?"

"No, and now that I think about it..." Charlie said, a frown crossing his brow, "maybe I should have told you about this."

"Go on."

"George said a stranger showed up at the ranch askin' if a certain person was on the coach. Pa sent George down to find out. Pa's always doin' favors for people."

"Yep, he's good at that," Cooper remarked knowingly. "Did George say if this person was on the coach?"

"He sure did. He said the man was real easy to spot. He had red hair."

Cooper let out a heavy sigh. Just as he'd thought, Patrick Doyle wasn't in Brownsville to sleep, and Cooper also suspected the stranger at the Johnson Ranch was Detective Connelly. But why was he staying there? Did Zeke know the man? Zeke had influence outside of Brownsville, but did it extend all the way to the San Francisco Police Department.

"Do you think this is important, Sheriff?"

"Yeah, Charlie, It could be."

"Do you want me to go back to the ranch and find out who it is?"

"Nope. I'll ride out there myself. I need to talk to your pa about those possible rustlers, and I should take another look around to see if there's any sign of them. I'm sure I'll meet this stranger when I'm there. Until then I'm not makin' any guesses. Remember that. Don't make any snap judgements. Always learn as much as you can before you come to any kinda conclusion."

"I can see that," Charlie said thoughtfully.

"Speaking of makin' sense, are you sure you wanna sleep in that office? Aren't you worried about the rats?"

"I'll have my gun, Sheriff. If a rat shows up I'll just shoot him."

"You're that good a shot?"

"My pa says I've got a better eye than a gunslinger."

Cooper smiled a wry smile. The same had been said about him once, but it had been said with dread.

CHAPTER TWENTY-FOUR

Sitting around the dinner table at the Johnson ranch, Zeke's sons had been peppering Frank Connelly with questions. To have a detective from the San Francisco police force in their home was intriguing, and the dramatic stories he'd been telling about life in the big city had captured their imaginations.

"Sure is a shame Charlie isn't here," Zeke's wife remarked. "He would've enjoyed all this. He's decided he wants to be a sheriff."

"So your husband told me," Frank said. "It's good he knows what he wants."

"He's a fine boy," Zeke declared, "but he can go a lot further. I was thinkin', Frank, once this business is over, how would you feel about showin' him around your offices. He's never been to the city. I could take him, and he could see the kinda life he could have as a policeman. He's got a fine brain."

Placing his fork on his plate, Frank looked across at his host and nodded his head, but not just in agreement. Now he understood why a total stranger had brought him into his home and sent his son into Brownsville to spy on the arriving stagecoach.

"I think that's a fine idea," Frank lied. "We're always looking for new recruits. I'll introduce him to the Captain and give him an idea of what a policeman in the city is up against. But if he wanted to join the force he'd have to start at the bottom."

"That's the way it should be. Work hard and make your way up, but it doesn't hurt to know the right people, eh, Frank?"

"No, it doesn't hurt. Where is this McTavish boarding house?" he asked, wanting to change the subject. "I want to swing by and see my sergeant tomorrow."

"It's down the first road before you enter the town. There's a thicket right there, you can't miss it," George interjected. "Um, I just remembered, your sergeant told the sheriff he probably wouldn't see much of him because he wanted to sleep for two days."

Zeke rolled his eyes. If Charlie had been the one to check out the coach, he would have remembered and reported every last detail.

"He was just bein' crafty," Frank said with a knowing smile. "He's been ordered to keep a low profile. Like I told your pa, I don't wanna scare this woman away."

"Oh, sure, yeah, I'll bet that's it," George said as if he knew what he was talking about. "Do you do that much? Pretend to be one person and you're actually someone else?"

"All the time, George," Frank replied, suppressing a wicked grin. "All the time."

* * *

At Ruby's home, Violet had finished her meal and placed the tray on the floor, then slipped from the bed and moved across to the vanity. Opening the small drawer on the right side of the oval mirror, she picked up a black velvet case, lifted the lid, and withdrew the diamond watch her dearest Earl had given her. She had no idea of its worth, but it glittered like the stars. Following his death she'd tried to pawn it, but the man who fenced the few pieces of jewelry she'd stolen, had told her he couldn't touch it.

"It's too unique. It would be identified in a heartbeat and I'd have big trouble on my hands, and, Violet, don't take it to anyone else."

"But I didn't steal this. It was given to me by Earl Wallace, and why shouldn't I try and pawn it if I can?"

"That detective has put the word out to all the pawnbrokers. If you show up they're to raise the alarm."

"But they don't know me. You're the only one I've ever done business with."

"His constables have given everyone your description, as best they can anyway, and that watch is famous. Everyone knows he gave it to you."

"How? I don't understand."

"You don't know? Earl's daughter. She had her sights on it, and one of the servants told her Earl had given it to you. From what I hear she was furious and said she was going to find you and get it back. No, you can't sell it, not in this town. Keep it safe though, it's worth a mint."

She remembered the conversation as if it was yesterday. She'd hated the thought of selling it, but she'd been thinking of the children the money would feed.

Sitting on the chair in front of the vanity, she felt a hot lump when she recalled the night Earl had given it to her. He'd been such a kind man. But now she had another kind man, a man she truly loved.

Placing it back in its case, Violet returned to the bed and slipped between the sheets. Night had fallen, a single lantern burned on the nightstand, and closing her eyes a soft smile crossed her face. Tomorrow she would be with Cooper in his bed. He would caress her and kiss her, but he'd said he had other things in store, and he'd made the promise with a very wicked smile.

"Other things," she murmured. "I wonder if you mean the kind of things Earl taught me about."

Her former lover had enjoyed tying her up and teasing her, blindfolding her, and feeding her chocolate and wine, but his most favorite other thing was placing her over his lap and spanking her. She'd loved it. She didn't know why, she just did, and the thought of her handsome sheriff doing the same thing made her toes curl.

"I can't wait," she muttered. "I absolutely can't wait."

It was only a moment later a mischievous grin crossed her lips.

She had a very naughty idea.

CHAPTER TWENTY-FIVE

Cooper woke up with a raging erection. Pushing back his bedcovers, he took hold of his member and stroked himself to a quick, powerful climax.

Violet hadn't just stirred his heart, she had woken the dark sexual creature inside him. It had been a long time since he'd been with someone who lit the kindling to his fire. Though he'd had plenty of playtime as a wild gunman, most of the women didn't enjoy his games, and he'd had no desire to engage with an unwilling partner. When he'd turned his life around and moved to Brownsville, he'd needed to prove himself worthy of the job. Now a devilish angel had sparked him to life and it felt good. It felt better than good.

Violet's flirtatious reaction to his threat of a spanking suggested she might be that rare breed of woman who loved surrendering to a take-charge lover. It was almost too much to hope for, but every instinct was telling him she was. He would know soon enough. In a matter of hours she would be in his bed.

He cleaned himself up and dressed for the day, then moved into his kitchen and cut himself a slice of apple pie one of the women had brought him. Preferring his morning coffee at his office, he washed it down with a cup of water, but as he was on his way to the front door he realized his house wasn't exactly sparkling. Taking a few minutes to pick up and wipe off the dirtier surfaces, he finally headed out and marched down the street.

He loved the day following a storm. The air was fresh, the houses looked clean, and there was no dust. The stores weren't yet open, and wondering if Charlie had shot any rats, he made a mental note to help the young man overcome his fear. Reaching his office he pushed the door, but came to an abrupt halt. Violet was sitting in the chair in front of his desk.

"Hello, Sheriff," she purred, standing up to greet him. "Isn't it a lovely morning?"

"Yes, it is a lovely morning," he repeated, astonished to see her. "What are you doing here, and where's Charlie?"

"Right here, Sheriff," Charlie exclaimed, walking in from the back. "I ended up on one of the cots. They're a bit more comfortable than the couch."

"I'm surprised you let your deputy sleep here," Violet remarked, and though pretending to disapprove, Cooper could see the mischievous sparkle in her eye.

"It was down to me, Miss Hamilton. The Sheriff was doin' me a favor."

"Charlie, I'm going to let you do the morning rounds!"

"You are? Dang!"

"Make sure you stop at every store window just like I showed you. Don't forget to walk around the back of the buildings to make sure no-one's passed out from drinkin' too much. If you find anyone, send them on their way. Take your time and do it right."

"I sure will, Sheriff," he replied, then grabbing his hat and wearing a happy smile, he headed out the door.

"So, Miss Hamilton," Cooper grinned, walking slowly towards her, "how can I be of service?"

"Sheriff, I'm here to turn myself in."

"I see. For what exactly?"

"You told me you'd have to spank me when I was better. I'm here for my punishment."

In spite of his satisfying orgasm just a short while before, Cooper could feel his cock stirring back to life.

"I see," he muttered. "Walk through that door."

"You're not going to do it here?"

"You'll be punished in one of the cells," he said sternly, enjoying her genuine surprise. "Now go on ahead of me."

Violet hadn't expected him to take her into the jail area, and finding it slightly unnerving, she turned and walked ahead of him. Moving through the door she found herself in a surprisingly large room with four cells in a row, and dangling from a couple of hooks opposite were dark metal rings holding oversized keys.

"Into the last cell by that back door," Cooper ordered. "Place your hands on the wall and scoot your feet back."

The night before Violet had been tantalized by the idea of surprising him at his office and asking for her punishment, but now butterflies had burst to life in her stomach, and she was suddenly apprehensive.

"Cooper, you're not going to spank me hard, are you?"

"It's Sheriff," he said firmly, walking up to her and placing his arm around her waist, "and I'll spank as hard as I think I should. Now it's time for you to tell me why I'm gonna heat up your butt."

"For purposely changing the subject when I don't want to talk about something," she said hastily. "I'm sorry about that, truly I am."

"Yep, and I'm also gonna spank you for bein' way too sassy."

"But I'm not—"

A solid slap stopped her mid-sentence, and with a loud yelp she darted surprised eyes over her shoulder.

"Best not to argue with me while I'm slappin' your backside."

"Yes, Sheriff."

A warm flood was seeping through her sex, and turning her eyes back to the wall she took in a long breath. Her mischievous adventure was turning out to be more exciting, more salacious, more frightening, more *everything*, than she'd ever imagined.

"I told you the first spankin' would be over your dress, and the second over my knee with your skirt up. That's what you're gonna get, but if you give me any lip those drawers will be down and I'll be reddening your naked bottom. Understand?"

"Yes, Sheriff."

* * *

As he tightened his hold, and smoothed his palm over her curves, he heard her gasp. She'd been craving his hot hand as much as he'd been yearning to deliver it, and as he began to smack her with a steady rhythm, his semi-erect cock sprang to full attention.

"Ow, ow, oh, Sheriff, ow, ow."

"You're not complainin' are you?"

"No, Sheriff," she said breathlessly. "I can't help it."

"Let's see if that's true. I'm gonna give you three hard swats on each cheek. If you make a single sound, I'll pull your dress up and bare your bottom."

Cooper grinned.

She could remain quiet if she wanted to, but would she?

CHAPTER TWENTY-SIX

He landed the first, then the second, and on the third she let out a yelp. Immediately lifting her skirt and throwing it over her waist, he reached around the front of her drawers, untied the string, and let them fall down her legs.

"Sheriff...oh, my goodness! Please don't!"

Ignoring her protest he grabbed her wrist, plonked himself down on the cot, pulled her over his lap and began lustily spanking her wonderfully round cheeks. He was smacking her hard, carrying his slaps from her sit spot to the center of her cheeks and back down again.

And as she wriggled he could see her glistening pussy.

He paused, slipping his fingers inside her, and as she moaned and squirmed against his hand, he twirled his finger around her clit.

"Sir, oh, Sir, don't stop, please don't stop."

"You forget who you're talkin' to," he growled, pulling his hand away. "Now you're gonna have to wait some more."

The spanking resumed, though he paused every few slaps to tease her. But his cock was screaming for attention.

"On your feet," he ordered, helping her up, "now turn around and grab the bars."

As he guided her into position, she wrapped her fingers around the cold steel poles, but her skirt had fallen. Quickly dropping his trousers, he grabbed it to lift it back over her waist.

"Sheriff? Sheriff? Are you here?"

Charlie's urgent call startled them both, and with her eyes wide in alarm, Violet hastily yanked up her drawers.

"Make the coffee. I'll be right there," Cooper called back, hurriedly pulling up his trousers. "Here, darlin', the key to my house," he whispered, pulling it from his pocket and thrusting it into her hand. "First street past the saloon, turn right, and it's the green house, third on the left. I'll meet you there as soon as I can."

"Sheriff, there's a problem!"

"I'm comin'," he called back, grabbing one of the key rings from its hook and unlocking the back door.

"I can't believe this," she whispered as she stepped into the alley.

"We'll be laughin' about this one day."

"I already am," she giggled, then turned and hurried away.

Quickly locking the door and straightening the blanket over the cot, he took a deep breath and strode into the office, only to find Charlie sitting on top of a well-built man lying on his stomach.

"Charlie...what the blazes...?"

"I was checkin' behind the stores like you said, and caught him tryin' to pick the lock on the back door of the bank. He came with me okay, but when we walked in here he threw a punch. I ducked and got him in the gut."

"Good work!" Cooper exclaimed, helping to pull the man up to his feet, but studying his face, Cooper shook his head. He'd never seen the man before.

"Who are you?" he demanded. "Whatta you doin' in Brownsville? Are you here alone?"

"I'm not sayin' nothin.'"

"Do you like to eat?" Cooper growled.

"Huh? Whatta ya mean?"

"If you like to eat you'd better start talkin' or I'll have my deputy remove your front teeth—with his knuckles."

"You wouldn't! You can't do that!"

"Says who?"

"It's just wrong. The law don't allow for that!"

"This is my town! My laws! My justice. Besides, do you see any witnesses here? I'd just say you lost your front teeth threatenin' my life."

"Let me Sheriff," Charlie growled. "Nothin' could start my day off better."

"Okay, okay," the man said hastily. "There were four of us. We were gonna get us some cattle but it wasn't so easy. The other three took off, but I decided to stick around and see if maybe I could score at the bank."

"Why'd you do it at this time of day?"

"I've done it before and it worked."

"Lock him up."

As Charlie pushed the man through the door to the cells, Cooper walked across to the small stove and made the coffee. He could hear Charlie cursing at the man, then the slam of the cell door.

"What happens now?" Charlie asked as he walked back in.

"I'll telegraph the sheriff over in Peabody. He'll have him picked up and he'll be tried in the courthouse over there. It's time Brownsville got its own."

"Why don't we have one?"

"The town hasn't been big enough, but I reckon we're pretty close to gettin' there now. Regardless, you did real good, Charlie."

"Thanks, Sheriff. What took so long for you to come into the office? Did somethin' happen out back?"

"The rat made a reappearance," Cooper replied, the idea coming on the spur of the moment. "I had a helluva time."

"I thought I heard somethin' when I came in. Uh, Sheriff."

"Yeah, Charlie?"

"You called me your deputy."

"You are unofficially. You've still got a ways to go, but you'll do just fine. I need to take off, probably be about an hour. I'll be at my house if it's urgent, but only if it's urgent."

"Okay. Anything you want doin'?"

"Sit on the porch and write down every detail about what happened with that joker, but keep lookin' up and watching the street. Make note of anything that strikes you...and especially any strange faces. Got it?"

"Sure thing, Sheriff."

"I'm real proud of you, Charlie. Real proud. Coffee's on, and I'll be back in a bit."

Stepping outside Cooper let out a long, heavy breath. It had been a close call, but striding down the street towards his house he broke into a broad grin. In spite of the alarming interruption he considered the morning a resounding success. He'd guessed right. Violet did share his love of the darker side of sex, and she was waiting for him at his house, possibly even lying in his bed. Wishing he'd thought to change his sheets, he quickened his pace.

CHAPTER TWENTY-SEVEN

Violet had giggled all the way to Cooper's house, but once safely inside she realized just how reckless they'd been. She was surprised. Cooper didn't strike her as reckless, though he'd made love to her without reservation after knowing her only a short time. She'd done the same, but her entire life had been unconventional. She grabbed hold when fleeting moments of happiness crossed her path. Throughout her life fleeting moments had been all she'd known.

Did Cooper have a similar history?

Perhaps they were more alike than she thought.

Looking around the living room it was obvious his home was merely a place to hang his hat, but the house was comfortable. After being exposed to some lovely homes during her days with Earl, she could see its potential. Ambling into the hallway she found two bedrooms, the larger of which was obviously his, and staring at the bed a naughty smile crossed her lips. Closing the curtains, she slipped out of her clothes and slid between the sheets.

As she settled in she relived the shocking moment when he'd bared her backside, yanked her over his lap and started spanking her. She'd been embarrassed, which had surprised her, and his hand had been rough, and a whole lot harder than Earl's.

But the entire episode had sent thrilling sparks through her entire being.

She loved his hard muscled body, his control, his easy authority, and how it was coupled with tenderness and compassion. His sexy smell was on the pillow, and inhaling deeply, she closed her eyes as a tingle rippled through her sex.

"Is this what it means to fall in love?" she whispered. "It has to be."

The sound of the front door snapped her from her thoughts. She realized he was probably expecting her to be naked and in his bed, and she wanted to surprise him with something more, but she had only seconds.

* * *

Cooper was confounded.

He'd had no intention of ravaging Violet in the cell.

It had been foolhardy at best.

Marching to his house he chided himself.

"What the blazes were you thinkin'?" he muttered. "You're not that wild outlaw anymore."

But as he turned the block and saw his house, it struck him.

He was.

The crazy cowboy who feared nothing and no-one, who by all accounts should be dead and buried, had only been sleeping, and the beautiful young woman with the mesmerizing green eyes had woken him up.

The epiphany rattled through his soul.

Her erotic assault in her room at the boarding house had startled him, but it hadn't stopped him making love to her.

Her conniving nature had turned him on, not turned him off.

She hadn't protested his ardent attack in the cell, and she'd been just as aware of the potential danger as he had.

She'd spent her life taking risks as he'd once done—was now doing again!

They were two peas in a pod!

His pulse had ticked up, and entering his house he wasn't surprised to find the living room empty. He'd already assumed the naughty girl would be waiting between the sheets. Making sure to lock the front door, he walked quickly to his bedroom, but as he entered he broke into a broad grin and shook his head.

Violet had used her stockings to tether her ankles to the bed frame at the foot of the bed, and had tied her chemise around her eyes as a blindfold.

"Well, well, what do we have here?" he murmured, his cock springing to life as he moved across to her. "A helpless female waitin' to be taken."

"Some villains came in through the window and did this to me, but when they heard you come in they ran away. Won't you please untie me and take off this blindfold?"

He had to chuckle. Her hands were free, but playing along he leaned over and whispered in her ear.

"You're stayin' just as you are, and I'm gonna take full advantage."

"No, you can't," she whimpered. "Please won't you—"

But his mouth had abruptly covered hers.

Grabbing her breasts, he kneaded them roughly as he crushed her lips, then breaking away he unknotted the kerchief around his neck and quickly tied her wrists.

"Now you really are helpless," he remarked as he removed his clothes, "and I think I'm gonna tease you for a while. Make sure you're nice and wet when I slide my big cock in you."

Her whimpered moan and salacious wriggle made him grin, and sitting on the edge of the mattress he touched his fingertip to her slick slit.

"Looks like you're already in the mood. Did one of those villains mess with you?"

"He did, he put his mouth on my titties and fingered me."

"I should thank him for warmin' you up, and I'm gonna take the same liberties."

Dropping his mouth to her breasts, he slowly drew in each nipple, sucking hungrily as he sent his hand between her legs. Her moans grew louder, and he thrust his finger into her depths, searching out the magic spot deep inside her channel. Gently pressing, he was rewarded with a wail of pleasure, then carefully pulling it out, he rose to his feet.

* * *

Violet was beside herself. She hadn't expected him to tie her wrists and she felt truly helpless. When he had sucked on her breasts like a starving vampire, waves of scintillating sensations had coursed through her body, and as his fingers began to explore her sex, she thought she would faint from pleasure. Now she'd felt him leave the bed, and she had no idea where he'd gone, or if he was even still in the room.

"I'm untyin' your stockin's, and you're gonna roll over, get on your knees and rest on your elbows. I want your ass high."

"Yes, Sheriff."

She would be in a lewd position, and as she felt him release her ankles, her heart began to hammer, and a fresh wave of butterflies burst to life in her stomach.

"Go on, be quick about it. I don't like to be kept waitin.'"

He was being gruff, acting out the part, and it was fueling her fever. Shifting on the bed, she did her best to follow his instructions, but his hands unexpectedly clutched her waist and began moving her into position.

"Arch your back," he exclaimed, landing a hot slap, "arch it good and spread your legs."

Feeling him climb up behind her she waited for his cock, but he had other plans. His hands gripped her cheeks and pulled them apart. A hot flame burned her across her face, and she thought she would die from humiliation, but his lecherous display of her most private part was cursory.

"That was to show you I'm the boss of your body," he declared, moving his hands to grasp her hips, "and I'm gonna help myself to every bit of it."

His cock was sitting at her entrance mercilessly teasing her, and as she bucked back begging him to thrust inside her, though he didn't pull away, he didn't accept her invitation either.

"You want somethin'?"

"You, please, you."

"Am I the boss of your body?"

"Yes, Sir."

"Lemme hear you say it."

"You're the boss of my body."

"Are you happy about that?"

"Yes," she panted, barely able to stand his salacious torment. "I am, I swear. I want you to be the boss of my body."

With agonizing slowness, he pushed inside her, and as he began to pump with strong measured strokes, she dropped her head into the covers and let out a long, low, endless moan.

He was possessing her.

She loved it.

And she loved him.

Totally and completely.

He had become the boss of her body and her heart.

CHAPTER TWENTY-EIGHT

Cooper heard her surrender in her bleating pleasure, and he could feel it in his soul. They were connecting on a level that transcended sex, and he knew they belonged together. They dared to defy convention, they seized opportunity and had the courage to risk, they lived with compassion and refused to be victims. They were two sides of the same coin, and submitting to the profound understanding, he drove his cock forward, accelerating with every stroke until he was pummeling her pussy. She suddenly cried out his name, then he heard her suck in the air. Her orgasm was seizing her, and as she erupted his climax gushed through his loins.

Wild tingles buzzed through his limbs, his heart was pounding against his chest, but he continued to thrust even as his convulsions waned. Her crescendo seemed to last forever, but as the last wave ebbed and she dropped on the bed, he slipped out and collapsed next to her. Still panting he rolled her on to her back, untied her wrists and removed her blindfold. As she breathlessly gazed into his eyes he saw the threat of tears.

"Hey," he panted, pulling her into his arms. "Easy, darlin', what's wrong?"

"I'm s-so happy and s-so s-scared," she stammered. "Hold me."

"Whatta you scared of?" he asked softly, tightening his hug. "You worried about havin' a baby? I'm real sorry about that. It took me over. You make me crazy, Violet."

"No," she sniffled, "that doesn't scare me. It's you. It's me. I've never felt like this."

"Like what?" he asked huskily, pulling back and staring down at her. "Tell me."

"I love you. I love you with all my heart. I love you so much it hurts."

"I feel the same, Violet. I love you, darlin', and I swear I never thought I'd utter those words. But it's the God's honest truth. I reckon I lost my heart the moment I saw you by that stagecoach."

"Me too. You and your half-naked body."

Their lips met, and as happy tears spilled down her face, Cooper thought his heart would burst. Their kiss lingered, neither wanting it to end, but when they finally broke apart and were breathlessly snuggling together, Cooper let out a grunt.

"What was that?"

"That was me complainin'. I wanna stay with you but I've gotta send out a couple of telegrams, then ride out to Zeke Johnson's house. That fella Charlie caught was one of the rustlers and I need to tell Zeke what's goin' on."

"What a shame."

"Violet," he said hesitantly, "there's another reason I've gotta go out to the Johnson ranch. I don't wanna worry you, but I need you to keep your eyes open."

"I'm not going to like this," she mumbled under her breath.

"I reckon not. Charlie told me a stranger is stayin' there. Just appeared outta nowhere."

"Oh, no! You think it's Detective Connelly."

"I'm just sayin' keep your eyes open."

"You're leaving right now?"

"Yep, but before I go, tell me where you learned about bein' blindfolded and tied up? Who was he?"

"His name was Earl Wallace. He was a lovely man. We were going to be married."

"Dang, I wasn't expectin' that."

"I didn't feel for him the way I feel for you, but I cared for him deeply. He was quite a bit older than me. I met him on the tenth anniversary of his wife's passing. He was sitting on a park bench and he looked so sad. I wanted to cheer him up, so I sat next to him. We ended up having afternoon tea, and I don't know why, but I told him all about myself. The orphanage, running away, the children, everything. We started seeing each other, and I really liked being with him. He helped the children with clothes and food, and he was always a gentleman. But he often joked about spanking me, and I started to find it intriguing. When he finally did, I loved it. Soon after that he asked me to marry him. We were happy together, though he had a daughter who was very jealous. She didn't like me one bit, but he didn't care. He said I made him feel like a new man, and I believe I did."

"What happened?"

"One night at dinner he gave me a beautiful watch. He said it meant more than the engagement ring he was going to buy me. I was moving from my lodgings to stay at his house the next day, and he was going to his lawyer's office to work out his will so I'd never want for anything. We kissed goodbye, and that was the last time I ever saw him. He had a heart attack overnight and passed away."

"No! Violet. You must've been devastated."

"Those were dark days, Cooper. Very dark days. I did try to sell the watch to a pawnbroker I knew, but he warned me that Detective Connelly had put the word out. I couldn't take it anywhere."

"Do you still have it?"

"The watch? Yes of course. It's very precious to me. I'm glad I didn't sell it now."

"I'm sure you are."

"There was one other man in my life," she said softly, "except he was a boy, not a man. His name was Jimmy. We ran away from the orphanage together. Things just happened between us. It was like breathing. Nothing special, but we were close."

"And what happened to Jimmy?"

"He got a live-in job working for this very wealthy family. He ran their errands, polished shoes, whatever they needed. He said he could get me a job there as a maid or working in the kitchen."

"You didn't take it?"

"Heavens no. I'd rather be dead than live a life of drudgery."

"How old were you?"

"Fifteen."

"You turned down three meals a day and a roof over your head?"

"I turned down prison."

"You're remarkable," he murmured, hugging her tightly. "You truly are one of the bravest people I've ever met."

"I doubt that."

"It's true, and I'm glad you told me all that. It explains a lot. Now we have to get dressed and I'll walk you back to Ruby's."

"Thank you for the best afternoon of my life. I'll never forget it."

"Neither will I," he said, kissing her softly.

It only took them a few minutes to dress, and stepping outside into bright sunshine, she looped her arm through his elbow as they started off. They had to walk down Main Street a short way, then cross over and down the block to Ruby's.

* * *

Standing outside Al's Mercantile, Hannah caught sight of a pretty young woman in a beautiful dress walking with the sheriff. It took a moment to notice the sheriff was grinning, and the lovely lady on his arm was laughing along with him.

Hannah suddenly realized they were a couple!

And she saw red.

CHAPTER TWENTY-NINE

After stopping at the telegraph office to contact the sheriff in Peabody, Cooper returned to the jailhouse to check in on Charlie and the bank robber. Walking in the door he found Charlie sitting at the desk, his head buried in the manual.

"Hey, Sheriff."

"Hey, Charlie. How's your prisoner?"

"Quiet as a mouse."

"I'm headin' off to your pa's ranch and I want you visible. Sit on the porch. That's why I whittle out there. People think I'm focused on the wood, and I am, but I've always got one eye on the street and one ear to the ground."

"I'll go out there right now."

"One more thing. Remember, don't talk to anyone about Rose Hamilton, or anything else we've discussed. Not a word to a soul. If anyone describes her, tell them she sounds like a lotta pretty girls in this town."

"You told me what we talk about is between you and me, and that's the way it'll stay. You don't have to worry, Sheriff."

"Worryin' is what I do, Charlie. It's good for business, but I know you'll do just fine. I'm goin' out to saddle up. Will your mare be all right by herself?"

"Sure. The Hobson's horses are nearby."

"I'll throw her some hay to keep her happy."

"Thanks, Sheriff."

"We'd be nowhere without our horses. Gotta treat 'em right."

Deciding to take the fastest route out the back door, as he passed by the cells he saw the thief snoozing on the cot.

"Probably a lot more comfortable than the hard ground," Cooper murmured as he passed, but when he looked at the empty cell where he'd spanked Violet, he couldn't suppress a grin. The unexpected interruption would be a moment they'd be laughing about for many years to come.

"Many years to come," he muttered, repeating his thoughts as he strode across the alley to the corral and small barn. "I've gotta get my head around this."

His horse walked up to the fence as Cooper neared, and opening the gate he rubbed his neck, then headed into the barn to throw on the saddle. River followed him like a puppy, and Hazel followed River.

"You've gotta stay put, girl, but here's some hay. That'll keep you happy for a bit."

Cooper tacked up River while the mare stood nearby enjoying the snack, and barely flicked an ear as he led his horse out the gate and mounted up. As he rode down Main Street he returned the friendly waves of passersby, but when he smiled at Hannah, she scowled at him and flounced away. Barely giving it a second thought, he was soon leaving the town behind and cantering across the open fields towards Zeke Johnson's ranch.

Climbing a hill and reaching a plateau, he pulled his horse to a stop and took in the view below. His town looked serene, but as a cool breeze rustled around him he felt a ripple of apprehension. The ominous feeling that had shivered through him a couple of times was back, and he abruptly felt an urgent need to reach the Johnson home.

Kicking River forward, he galloped up the rest of the gentle slope, and as he descended into the valley below, the sprawling ranch house came into view. It was only a few minutes later he was approaching the homestead, and spotted George chopping wood, no doubt storing up for the coming winter. Like Charlie, he was a big lad, and all muscle.

"Hey, Sheriff," George said as Cooper pulled to a stop and climbed off. "Whatta you doin' out here?"

"I need to talk to your pa. Is he in?"

"Sure is. Go ahead. I'll get your horse some water."

"Much obliged."

Striding up to the front door, he banged the iron ring on its metal plate. It was quickly answered by Millicent, Zeke's wife. She always had a smile on her face, which Cooper found surprising considering she had four sons, a large house, and a husband to take care of. He couldn't begin to imagine the work involved.

"Sheriff! Come on in. It's good to see you. Can I get you some coffee?"

"That'd be welcome. Thanks, Mrs. Johnson."

"Zeke! It's the sheriff," she called, but receiving no response she shook her head and tutted. "It's this house. It's too big. He must be in our bedroom. I'll go and fetch him. Come through to the living room. I suppose you want to see your fellow lawman."

"Uh, yeah, since I'm here," Cooper replied, feeling his pulse tick up.

"Interesting fellow," she continued. "A bit citified for me, but Zeke seems to like him."

"Is he in the house?"

"Detective Connelly? No, he left a little while ago. Said he had a sergeant in town he needed to visit with."

"Sergeant Doyle?"

"That's him. Sergeant Doyle. I guess he's here to search out that woman. Nasty business."

"I'm surprised he told you about it," Cooper remarked, hoping she'd continue talking. "Things like that are usually kept quiet."

"He told Zeke and Zeke told me. Do we have a murderess in our town, Sheriff? Have you seen her?'"

"No, I don't believe we do," he replied, doing his best to keep his voice even. "At least, not to my knowledge."

"I hope you catch her and catch her quick. Fancy killing an old man. It's terrible, just terrible."

"Who are you talkin' to, Millie?" Zeke asked as he strode into the room. "Oh, Sheriff. Howdy. What brings you here? Have a seat."

"I'll fetch that coffee," Millicent said, bustling away.

CHAPTER THIRTY

Cooper caught his breath.

Hearing Connelly was riding into town wasn't good news.

As Zeke settled into a chair, Cooper gathered his thoughts and sat down opposite him.

"I have some news about the rustlers and I was hopin' to meet the detective," Cooper began, "but your wife said he's gone into town to catch up with his sergeant."

"Yep. He left a while ago. I thought he'd be back by now. Maybe he got lucky and found that woman, but tell me about the rustlers."

"Charlie caught a man tryin' to break into the back door of the bank this mornin'. Turns out he was one of them."

"Good for Charlie. Millie will be real proud."

"There were four in all, but the other three took off, claimed it was too tough."

"After the problems over near Peabody I hired some more boys to keep lookout," Zeke declared. "I guess it paid off."

"Here's your coffee," Millicent said, entering the room carrying in a tray. "I've brought you some cake as well. I hope you like it."

Though Cooper was anxious to head back into town to find Connelly, he didn't want to appear rude, and picking up his mug he drank some of the coffee, then lifted the cake and took a large bite.

"This is real good, Mrs. Johnson."

"My wife knows her way around a kitchen," Zeke grinned, "and with all us men in the house it's just as well."

"I'm sure Detective Connelly is enjoyin' his stay," Cooper said, hoping for more information. "I'm sorry I missed him. Did he happen to mention how long he'd be here?"

"He said a couple of days, but it depends on whether he can find this woman he's been trackin'. Have you seen her?"

"I don't know what she looks like."

"He says she's real pretty with bright green eyes and reddish-brown hair, but he's tryin' to keep quiet about bein' here. He's worried if she gets wind of him and his sergeant she'll take off.

"Thinkin' on it, I should get back to town and see if I can find him," Cooper declared, rising to his feet. "Maybe I can help."

"Probably a good idea," Zeke agreed. "You can't miss him. Tall, with a big mustache, though like I said, I thought he'd be back by now."

"Maybe I'll pass him on my way into town. Thanks for the coffee and cake, Mrs. Johnson."

"Any time, Sheriff. I'll walk you out."

They made their way through the foyer to the front door, but as he stepped outside, a thought crossed his mind.

"Mrs. Johnson, in case I miss him, could you please tell the detective I was here."

"Of course."

"And tell him I said..."

"Yes, Sheriff?"

"I came to remind him about jurisdiction."

"Jurisdiction?"

"That's right. It means he can't come into my town and arrest people. He has to go through me."

"But if that woman is a murderess..."

"If...that's the key word, Mrs. Johnson. *If.* We can't believe everything people tell us. Has she been convicted? Maybe she's innocent. We don't know anything about this. I reserve judgment until all the facts are known."

"Landsakes. You're right, Sheriff. Thank you for saying that. And I'll be sure and pass on the message."

Walking across to River tied under the shade of a tree, Cooper waved to George, mounted up and rode off. To anyone watching he would have appeared calm, but he was deeply worried.

"Please, God, keep her safe," he muttered as he pushed River into a gallop. "Why the blazes did I leave town?"

* * *

Patrick Doyle was red-faced and sweating.

He'd been woken from a deep sleep by a loud banging.

Feeling as though he was on the verge of a heart attack, he jumped from his bed, and for a moment he didn't know where he was.

The banging happened again.

Realizing it was someone at his door he rushed to open it. Staring up at the scowling face of Detective Frank Connelly, he almost had a heart attack a second time.

"F-Frank," he stammered, stumbling backwards. "What are you doing here?"

"What are you doing sleeping in the middle of the goddamned day?" the detective retorted, pushing Patrick aside.

"The trip, it didn't sit well. I'm not feeling good."

"Have you started looking for Violet Parker?"

"Uh, no, like I said, I haven't been well."

"Get dressed. Here's a list of the other boarding houses. Go to Mrs. Elwood's first. It's at the other end of Main Street. Sounds like the kind of place that would appeal to her."

"But Frank—"

"Now!" the detective shouted. "When you're done there, start going into the shops. Ask questions and keep your eyes open. I'm heading into the saloon for a drink and talk with the girls. For the right price they'll tell me if they've seen her. If you have any news come and find me."

"Aren't you afraid she'll hear that you're in town?"

"I gave this a lot of thought last night and I'm changing tactics. We need to ask questions, bribe, threaten, coerce, do whatever it takes, and I want her to know I'm here. If she's scared she'll make a mistake. But if that doesn't work we'll pretend to leave, then I'll sneak back and find a way to lay low. The minute she shows herself I'll grab her. One thing I can tell you for sure. I'm not leaving this rinky-dink town without her. Now for fuck's sake, get dressed."

* * *

When Violet had returned to her room she'd kicked off her shoes and laid down. The morning had been thrilling, but exhausting. The strict but scintillating spanking, the unexpected interruption when she was in the cell with Cooper and her urgent escape, then making love at his home followed by their ardent confessions of love, had left her deliriously happy but very tired. Letting out a sigh, she closed her eyes and felt the weariness seep through her bones.

"I do love you, Cooper," she mumbled as she felt herself drift away. "After this nap I must think of a way to show you. Maybe I'll go to Al's and see what I can find for you. Yes, that's what I'll do. There's bound to be something."

* * *

Downstairs in the kitchen Ruby was humming as she baked. She was making a special dinner for Violet and the Sheriff. When Violet had returned from her morning walk she'd been positively beaming, and had confessed she and the sheriff were in love, then let out a long, heavy yawn.

Watching Violet walk slowly up the stairs, Ruby had almost cried with joy. If there was ever a man who deserved happiness it was Cooper. The minute the cake was out of the oven she was going directly to the Sheriff's office to invite him over for supper.

CHAPTER THIRTY-ONE

Fighting a rising panic, Cooper had galloped all the way back to town and made his way directly to the boarding house. Throwing the reins over the hitching post, he hurried up the path, pushed open the front door and urgently hurried inside.

"Ruby?"

"Goodness, Sheriff, is something wrong?" Ruby asked, stepping into the foyer.

"A detective from San Francisco is here chasin' after Rose. He may be a lawman but he's a bad fella. Has he been by?"

"No, he hasn't, thank the Lord. What should we do?"

"He could come stormin' through here and push his way into everyone's room. Until he's outta town I'm takin' Violet to stay at my house. All I can do is pray no-one see's her goin' in with me."

"My goodness, my goodness. Your house, yes, that's probably the best thing."

"I'm goin' up to get her packin."

"Is there anything I can do?"

"What about the other lodgers? They must know she's been here."

"Oh, dear, yes, they do. I'll have a private word with each of them the minute they get back."

"If this detective does show up, don't believe anything he or his sergeant tells you, and thank you."

"You don't need to thank me, Sheriff. Just take care of her."

"Don't worry about that," Cooper said solemnly. "I'll do whatever I must to keep her safe."

Taking the stairs two at a time, he hurried down the hall and tapped on her door. Not getting a response, he opened it up and peered inside. She was lying on her bed, eyes closed, softly sleeping. Walking quickly across the room he gently shook her awake.

"Cooper," she murmured with a sleepy smile. "You're back. Why do you look so worried? Oh, no, he's here!" she exclaimed, suddenly wide awake.

"Yep, and he's in town. I'm movin' you to my house. You'll be safe there."

"I'll get my things together," she replied, hastily slipping from the bed.

"I'll track him down, and make sure he's busy so I can get you over there without runnin' into him. I'll be back to get you as soon as things are under control."

"I'll be ready."

"It'll be okay," he said reassuringly, giving her a quick hug. "I swear I'll keep him away from you."

"I know you will, and I'm fine, honestly."

"If by chance he does cross your path, run to my office."

"Cooper, listen. Isn't that a man's voice?" she asked breathlessly.

Cooper had left the door ajar, and he could clearly hear a man speaking to Ruby.

"Lock the door," he whispered, then strode from the room and hurried to the landing. Peering into the foyer he saw the red-headed portly sergeant. Letting out a quick breath of relief, he trotted down the stairs.

"Mr. Doyle," he declared, marching forward with his shoulders squared, oozing authority. "I heard loud voices. Is this gentleman causing a problem, Mrs. Elwood?"

"Sheriff, I apologize," Patrick said hastily. "I should have introduced myself properly when we met. I'm a sergeant with the San Francisco police department, and I'm here about a young woman named Violet Parker."

"I told him I've never heard of her," Ruby declared, "but he's insisting I allow him into all the rooms. I won't have it, Sheriff. My guests have a right to their privacy."

"I'll handle this, Ruby. No-one will be going into any of your guest's rooms."

"Thank you, Sheriff," she said gratefully. "Now if you'll excuse me, I'll be going back to my kitchen. I have work to do."

"You go right ahead," Cooper said, shooting the unwelcome visitor a warning scowl.

The man's face was scarlet, and Cooper thought he looked as scared as a man facing down a rattler.

"Sheriff, I must insist—"

"Listen up, Sergeant Doyle, or whoever you are, this is *my* town. No-one, and I mean *no-one,* comes here and bullies my citizens. Got it!"

"AND YOU CAN TELL THAT DETECTIVE OF YOURS HE'D BETTER GET OUT OF HERE BEFORE I SHOOT HIM," Violet yelled, charging down the stairs, "AND I WILL IF I SEE HIM. BELIEVE ME, I WILL!"

Both men stared in shock as Violet reached the bottom and glared up at them.

"Violet!" Cooper said sharply, stunned she'd disobeyed him and was being so foolish, "you need to—"

"I'm tired of running. I'm tired of being accused of things I haven't done!" she exclaimed, cutting him off. "You listen to me Sergeant Doyle! That so-called detective of yours is an evil monster. Did you know he attacks the women he brings into his office for questioning? Did you know he rips off their clothes and forces himself on them? Did you know that? Did you know he steals everything they have? Did you know he's got a drawer where he keeps locks of their hair and their stockings and whatever jewelry they might have on when he drags them in there? Did you know he terrorizes them to within an inch of their lives? Did you know he makes the shopkeepers pay him money, and tells them if they don't he'll arrest them on some phony charge and ruin their lives? Did you know all that? If you did and you're working for him, you're as bad as he is, and if you didn't you do now, and you'd better do something about it! Enough is enough, Sergeant Doyle. That man should be hanged for the things he's done."

* * *

It had been an astonishing speech, and once she'd started Cooper wasn't about to stop her. Not only did she need to release her rage, he wanted to hear everything she had to say. When she'd finished he could scarcely believe what he'd heard, and it was obvious Patrick Doyle was dumfounded.

"Is this true?" the sergeant finally sputtered. "Is this really true?"

"No! I'm making it all up!" she snapped. *"Of course it's true!"*

"Sergeant, I reckon it's about time you started seein' things for what they are," Cooper said gravely. "That man is an evil snake and he's gotta be stopped."

"I don't know what to say," Patrick muttered, shaking his head. "Honestly, I'm speechless."

"Say you'll do something!" Violet retorted. "And I mean right away."

"I, uh, yes. Yes I will. Do you have a telegraph office here, Sheriff?"

"Sure do. Just a few doors down from Al's Mercantile. You can't miss it."

"Uh...before I go I must tell you something, Violet," he said sheepishly. "My wife, Erin Doyle, she does charitable works where you live, or used to live."

"That's your wife? People there think very highly of her."

"She thinks highly of you too. She didn't want me to come after you, but I had to follow orders. She thinks you're a saint, and she told me if I found you I had to leave you alone. I believed her, and I'd planned on staying a couple of days then heading home. I only visited this boarding house because the detective showed up and sent me here. He's hell-bent on finding you."

"That's because he's scared. He knows I'm going to tell the world who he really is and what he's been up to."

"Why would he know that?" Cooper asked, raising an eyebrow and looking at her solemnly.

"I might have, uh, mentioned it when I left him curled up on the floor of his office."

CHAPTER THIRTY-TWO

For a second time, both men were speechless and staring at her in shock.

"Violet, did you just say you left him curled up on the floor of his office?" Patrick finally asked.

"Uh, yeah."

"How exactly did that happen?" he pressed.

"His crotch fell into my knee!"

"So you defended yourself by assaulting his family jewels, then you threatened him," Patrick muttered with a deep frown. "Probably not the smartest thing you could've done."

"He attacked me! I had to get away!"

"Right, uh, sorry," Patrick apologized quickly. "I meant threatening him. That part. He doesn't take well to threats."

"Violet, go back to your room and start packin'," Cooper said firmly. "I'll be back in a little while. In the meantime, don't go anywhere."

"Okay. Sergeant Doyle, I'm sorry I barked at you just now."

"I can't say I blame you, and I'm glad you told me everything. It's time the truth came out."

"Thank you," she said softly, and as she headed up the stairs, both men silently watched her.

"I'm at a loss, Sheriff. I don't know what to do," Patrick said, lifting his cap and running his fingers through his mop of red hair.

"Are you lookin' for advice?"

"I guess I am. I believe her, and she's right, he has to be stopped, but crossing him, that's, uh..."

"Dangerous?"

"Yeah, that's dangerous. I don't think he's even supposed to be here. I was going to send the Captain a telegram, but I'm not sure if I should. Connelly will make my life a misery until I produce Violet, and if I go back, he'll be furious that I left. I can't even imagine what he'll do to me if I contact the Captain, let alone accuse him of everything Violet just told us."

"Where is he now?"

"He's at the saloon. He said he's going to question the girls—and he likes his whiskey."

"Lay low at your boarding house. I'll deal with Connelly, then I'll come by and give you an update."

"Thank you, Sheriff. It's all very tricky," Patrick added, shaking his head.

"Perhaps not as tricky as you think. I'll walk back with you as far as my office. I need to drop off my horse then I'm goin' to the saloon. I want those girls to keep him busy, and I'll also make sure he has too much to drink. That should stop him causin' any trouble for a while."

"That will be a relief. When I think about those poor women and those shopkeepers it makes me sick."

"Yeah, it's bad. I want you to do me one favor though."

"Whatever you need."

"I don't know how this is gonna play out, but if you do contact your Captain, don't mention the drawer where Connelly keeps his ill-gotten gains."

"But that will prove what Violet told me is true. The Captain will need to see it."

"I know, and that's why it's gotta be handled the right way. You leave that with me. I don't wanna say more than that right now, but trust me, Frank Connelly's evil days are over."

"I wish we'd met under better circumstances, Sheriff. I'd enjoy working for someone like you."

"Mighty kind of you to say. If you ever get a notion to move outta the city I can promise you a job."

"Are you serious?"

"I sure am. Brownsville is growin', and all I've got is a kid for a deputy. I could use a man with your experience."

"I might just talk to Erin about that," Patrick said thoughtfully.

"Bye, Ruby. I'm leavin'," Cooper called down the hall, "but I'll be back in a bit."

"Bye, Sheriff," she said, bustling out of her kitchen. "I'm taking a cup of tea upstairs. I want to check on our girl."

"Good idea. Thanks. Are you ready Patrick?"

"I sure am. Goodbye, Mrs. Elwood, and my apologies for disrupting your day."

"Your apology is accepted. Goodbye, Mr. Doyle."

Walking them to the door she closed it behind them, and her head still spinning with all she'd heard, she returned to the kitchen to set the kettle to boil.

* * *

Violet was pacing.

She'd never exploded in her life, but once she'd started she couldn't stop. Years of pent-up frustration and fury had burst out of her, and when she'd finished she almost felt sorry for the shocked sergeant who had been the target of her rage. He'd been cherry-faced and confounded, then full of remorse and empathy. But the episode had left her full of restless energy. She knew she needed to pack, but she could only march around the room.

"I thought you might like a cup of tea."

Turning around, she saw Ruby walking in carrying a cup and saucer. She hadn't even heard the door open.

"We're English at heart," Ruby said softly, "and my mother always made me a cup of tea if I was upset."

"You heard?"

"Hard not to—Violet."

"I'm sorry. I had to use a different name."

"I know, and I can understand why, and now you're all wound up. Sit down and drink this. It will help."

"Thank you," Violet said gratefully, taking the tea and perching on the edge of her bed. "You've been so kind. I feel terrible that I lied to you."

"You don't have to apologize. Like I said, it's understandable, but when I think about what you've been through! Where is your family?"

"My parents died within a month of each other when I was about six. They had some kind of lung disease, both of them, and I was taken to an orphanage."

"But what about your relatives? Was there no-one?"

"My father and mother had to break from their families in order to marry. I was born in England, but things became so difficult they broke all ties and came here to start a new life. They weren't in touch with anyone."

"How tragic. Were they very poor?"

"Poor? My goodness, no. My father was some kind of noble. That was the problem. His family was furious that he was marrying a commoner, and my mother's family turned nasty and began demanding all kinds of things because my father was rich. It was a mess, or so I was told. I was very young when they explained it all."

"Then surely there must have been money set aside for you."

"I do remember my father telling me there was, but any documents were sent with me to the orphanage, but I ran away, so I have no idea what happened to them, let alone any kind of inheritance. I assume someone at that place got their hands on it. They were awful people. Just awful."

"Does the Sheriff know about this?"

"Not yet, but I plan on telling him."

"You must! Inquiries can be made."

"I'm sure it's all been lost or stolen."

"But my dear, you don't know that. You must check."

"Someone else said that once. He was going to look into it, but he had a heart attack before he could. I would love to know what happened to my parent's belongings. I only have one small photograph. Perhaps with Cooper's help I might be able to find out. Yes, I will. I will make inquiries."

"I always knew you were a lady," Ruby said thoughtfully. "There's just something so elegant about you."

"Me? Elegant?"

"You're gracious without trying to be. There's a saying. Give me a child until he is seven, and I will give you the man. Until you were six years old you were raised by a gentleman, and I'm sure your mother was a lovely woman."

"From the little I remember, she was, and you're so kind to say so, Ruby."

"I'm just speaking the truth, and I have no doubt whatever you did to survive, you did it with style."

"Right now the only thing I need to do is make sure that beast of a man doesn't catch me."

"You'll be safe at the sheriff's house."

"Ruby, I pray you're right. I truly pray you're right."

CHAPTER THIRTY-THREE

Leading his horse, Cooper started walking down Main Street with Patrick Doyle, but worried about Connelly, Patrick hurried away to the outskirts of town and the safety of the boarding house. Cooper watched the frightened man scurry away, then glancing up to the sheriff's office, he was pleased to see Charlie seated on the porch.

"Hey, Sheriff," Charlie said, jumping to his feet as Cooper approached.

"That was good. You looked like you were readin' but you saw me."

"It's not hard to stay alert while you're doin' something else. I never knew that."

"Nope, it's not. Listen up. I need you to take care of River for me. I'm goin' to the saloon. That detective from San Francisco is there—and Charlie— he's a real bad guy."

"Huh. Thanks for the warnin'. What will you do?"

"Beside's makin' sure he stays in there for a bit, I'm not sure. He can't arrest anyone in this town without my cooperation and he probably thinks he'll get it, but he's wrong. No tellin' what he'll do when he finds out. But I've got an iron in the fire that'll put him outta business, and I need him to stick around until tomorrow. "

"How will you keep him here?"

"I've got a few ideas, but I need to size him up before I do anything. After you finish with River stay on that porch and keep your eyes peeled and your ears listenin'. I might need you."

"Sure thing, Sheriff."

Leaving River in Charlie's capable hands, Cooper walked back down the street and entered the saloon.

He spied Frank Connelly the minute he entered.

The slick detective had a half-empty bottle of whiskey in front of him, and he was carousing with the girls. Cooper began ambling forward, surprised the detective didn't notice him.

"Well, howdy, Sheriff," the girl said with a sassy smile.

"The sheriff! Is that right?" Connelly declared, jerking his head up. "I stopped by your office but the kid there said you weren't around. Kind of young for a deputy. He wasn't even wearing a badge."

"And you are...?" Cooper asked, placing his hands on his hips as he stared down at him.

"Did I forget to introduce myself? My apologies. I'm Detective Frank Connelly from San Francisco."

"Welcome to Brownsville. Detective or not, you need to know my laws. I don't put up with brawlin' in the bar or fightin' in the street. Cheat at poker and you'll be locked up for a week then run outta town. Mess with any of my citizens and you won't get to try it a second time. Enjoy your stay."

"Whoa, hold on there, Sheriff," Frank exclaimed as Cooper turned to walk away. "I need a chat."

"I'm a busy man, Detective," Cooper said brusquely, pleased his charade of pretending to leave had worked so well. "Is it important?"

"I didn't come all the way from San Francisco to talk about the weather."

"Sounds like you want to talk privately. Wait for me in that quiet corner over there," Cooper ordered, pointing to a table across the room. "I need a word with one of the girls and I'll be with you when I'm done."

As Cooper walked to the bar, he could feel Connelly's eyes on him. The detective had been expecting a small town sheriff in awe of a big city police officer. Not only had he confounded Connelly, he'd taken control.

"Hey, Sheriff," Josie said, greeting him with a warm smile.

"Hey, Josie. Has that fella been lookin' for information?" he asked quietly.

"Yep. No-one's said a word, but one of the girls might be thinkin' on it. Maybe she saw something I don't know about."

"Tell her if she gives out any information she'll be spanked on her bare butt every night for a week, and spendin' those same nights in a cell. Be sure to add that I have ways of findin' these things out."

"That'll keep her quiet. Is there anything else I can do?"

"Yep, and I promise I'll reward you as soon as I can. I don't have any money on me right now."

"You know what I'd rather have," she twinkled.

"Behave or you'll be the one over my knee."

"Promise?"

"Josie! Can we get down to business?"

"That's what I'm hopin' for."

"This is serious," he said sternly. "Listen up."

"Sorry, Sheriff. Go ahead."

"I don't want that man to leave here for at least an hour, longer if you can manage it, and when he does step outside, I want him fallin' down drunk."

"I'll do my best, but he looks like a fella who can down a bottle and stay upright."

"What about that homemade brew of Kitty's? Doesn't that pack a wallop?"

"Yeah! It does! A few glasses of that stuff would knock out a horse."

"I have an idea. It's clear, right?"

"Yep."

"I'll be havin' a chat with him. Bring two glasses, but make mine water. The minute I've finished it, bring two more. He'll try to keep up with me."

"You are one sly devil."

"When I need to be, and this is one of those times," he replied with a wink.

"You go on over, Sheriff. I'll be right there."

As Cooper had directed, Connelly had moved to the far corner of the room. His compliance was a testament to the man's desperate need to find Violet. Cooper also believed Connelly served only one Master. His own demonic greed.

"How can I help you, detective?" Cooper asked as he approached.

"Why don't you take a seat? Care to quench your thirst?"

"Sure, but not whiskey," Cooper replied, raising his hand to Josie and showing two fingers. "I've just ordered us a real drink, and here it comes. Thanks, Josie. That was quick."

"You always order the same thing, and I figured you'd wanna share it," she said as she placed the glasses on the table. "Should I wait to get you a second?"

"May as well. Here's to your visit, Detective Connelly," Cooper said, lifting his glass and watching Connelly lift his. "Welcome to Brownsville. Bottom's up."

Splashing back the water in two swallows, Cooper had a hard time suppressing his laughter. The detective's face was bright red, and his hand flew to his chest.

"Damn, that's firewater!" he stammered, taking in several deep breaths.

"Too much for you, Detective?"

"Hell, no. I just have to get used to it. Bring me another as well."

"Make it two each, Josie," Cooper said with a wink. "That should keep us right for a few minutes."

"Okay, Sheriff."

"So what do you need from me, Detective Connelly? Why are you here?"

"There's a young woman in this town and I need to take her back to San Francisco."

"There are a lotta young women in this town. Who exactly?"

"Her name is Violet Parker, but she's probably using an alias."

"What does she look like?"

"Here are two more," Josie declared, returning quickly and placing the glasses on the table, "and a third."

"Thanks," Cooper said, delighted with her initiative. "Here's to law and order!"

Again he picked up the glass and downed it, obligating Connelly to follow suit.

"Fuck! What is this stuff?" Connelly sputtered, grabbing his throat. "I swear it's stripping the skin off my innards."

"Like you said, it takes gettin' used to, and you were sayin'?" Cooper pressed, lifting the third glass and sipping the water.

"Uh, yeah. She's got long reddish brown hair and green eyes. She's a liar and a thief and she killed a man."

"I assume you've got an arrest warrant."

"A what?"

"An arrest warrant. Cheers," Cooper added, clinking the third glass against Connelly's.

As the detective raised his tumbler and took another swallow, Cooper let out a relieved breath. He could see the home-made liquor was starting to kick in, though on top of half-a-bottle of whiskey it wasn't surprising. Violet could soon be safely moved, and Patrick Doyle's whereabouts would be the last thing on Connelly's mind.

"You don't need to worry about that, Sheriff," Connelly grunted, slurring his words. "The arrest warrant thing? It doesn't matter."

"I can't be lettin' you haul someone away without it. Wouldn't be right. Besides, I haven't seen this Viola."

"Violet! Not Viola, Violet. But like I said, I don't know what she's calling herself."

"It doesn't matter. Even if she was here under an assumed name I wouldn't just hand her over to some stranger who claims to be a detective. For starters I need verification from your office that you are who you say you are."

"What?"

"Come back and see me when you've got what I need," Cooper said rising to his feet. "I'll keep my eyes open, but people come through here all the time. I'll be seein' ya."

CHAPTER THIRTY-FOUR

Confident the evil detective wouldn't cause any trouble for a while, Cooper turned and started to walk away, but a loud crash made him spin around. Connelly was on his feet, and Cooper saw the man had smashed a glass against the wall behind him

"She's here and I fucking want her!" Connelly yelled. *"If you know where she is you'd better hand her over or you'll be sorry!"*

"Don't be raisin' your voice to me," Cooper said calmly.

"I'll raise my damn voice whenever and wherever I damn well please!"

"Ah, you're a mean drunk. I should've known," Cooper remarked, moving towards him. "I was hopin' you'd just pass out."

The saloon had fallen quiet.

Everyone was captivated by the scene playing itself out.

Not taking his eyes off the detective, Cooper raised his hand.

"Josie? Come over here...slowly."

"Yeah, Sheriff?" she asked, moving cautiously to his side.

"Go get Charlie for me."

"Sure, right away."

"Fifty-fucking-dollars to anyone who brings me Violet Parker! Long red hair. Green eyes. Get her here now and the money's yours!" Connelly bellowed, then slammed his fist on the table. *"Now! Get her here now!"*

"Frank Connelly, I'm arrestin' you for disturbin' the peace."

"What? The fuck you are!" Frank yelled, but as he wildly waved his arms in protest, he lost his balance, stumbled backwards and tumbled to the floor.

"You'll be spendin' the night in one of my cells," Cooper continued, standing over him with his hands on his hips. "You'd best cooperate or you'll be the one lookin' sorry."

"Who the hell do you think you are?" the detective grunted as he tried to stand up. "You're just a rinky-dink sheriff in a rinky-dink town?"

"And you're a drunk who needs to sleep it off."

It was only a moment later Charlie ran into the saloon. Hearing the shouts he'd already been on his way, and moving quickly to Cooper's side, he stared down at the man floundering on the floor.

"He's all arms and legs," Charlie muttered. "How are we gonna get him across the street?"

"Carefully," Cooper replied. "We'll start by usin' the handcuffs. If he starts swingin' those arms around he'll likely get one of us. Roll him over and—"

"Uh, sorry, I didn't bring them...or anything like that."

"Better run back and get 'em. Never arrive at a disturbance without handcuffs. Don't worry, you'll learn, and he's not goin' anywhere."

* * *

Out on the street, Hannah had been listening to the ruckus, and she was startled to see Charlie burst out of the saloon, dash into the sheriff's office, then run back out carrying shackles.

"What's going on, Charlie?" she called as he jogged past.

"A detective from San Francisco. He's blind drunk. We've gotta put him in a cell."

"What was that shouting about a woman and fifty dollars?"

"He was just mouthin' off. Sorry, can't stop."

Hurrying back into the saloon, he discovered Cooper had Connelly on his stomach and was holding his hands at the small of his back. Handing him the cuffs, he watched the sheriff deftly lock them around the man's wrists.

"He'll be hangin' off his cot," Charlie remarked as they pulled him to his feet. "He's as tall as a tree."

"As tall as a short tree," Cooper chuckled.

With the strong liquor kicking in, the detective was almost ready to pass out, and all they had to do was support him as they crossed the street and entered the sheriff's office. Pushing him through the door and into the first cell, Cooper felt a surge of satisfaction as he clanged the door shut.

"I guess we won't have to worry about him tonight," Charlie said as he watched the lanky detective flop on the cot.

"Nope, but tomorrow will be another story. If he wakes up and starts yellin', just leave him be 'til I get here."

"Okay, Sheriff."

"Now run over to McTavish's Boarding House," Cooper said as they walked back into the office. "Ask for a man by the name of Patrick Doyle. Tell him Connelly is locked up and will be stayin' in a cell overnight."

"Will do. Where will you be if I need you?"

"Mrs. Elwood's, then my house."

"Thanks, Sheriff. Sorry about forgettin' the handcuffs."

"No harm done, and a lesson learned."

"Seems to me I should just have 'em with me all the time."

"I don't have to use them much, but that's good thinkin'. I'm movin' Violet to my house until that lanky lizard is outta here, then I'll be off to see your pa again to let him know what's goin' on."

"Okay, Sheriff. I'll have River saddled and ready."

Feeling greatly relieved, Cooper started walking quickly down Main Street. Things had worked out even better than he'd planned, and he was looking forward to telling Violet her evil enemy was behind bars.

He couldn't wait to have her in his home, but she'd be sleeping with a hot backside. In spite of how things had worked out with Patrick Doyle when she'd confronted him, she should have stayed in her room. Her reckless action could have ended with a very different result.

And there was still another problem to figure out.

How to get Connelly out of town in the morning, and make sure he stayed gone, but passing the telegraph office an idea popped into his head. He paused, then smiled, and stepped inside.

* * *

When Hannah had seen Cooper leave his office, she wanted to run after him and ask about the drama in the saloon, but he ducked into the telegraph office.

She waited, then continued to follow along from the other side of the street. When he turned the corner, she paused to watch.

He walked halfway down the block, then entered Mrs. Elwood's Boarding house. Within minutes he emerged with the copper-haired, pretty woman at his side, and he was carrying a bag.

Hoping it meant he was taking her to the stagecoach depot and she was leaving town, Hannah was dismayed to see the happy couple turn in the opposite direction and start down the street where the sheriff lived.

Hurrying after them, she stared in disbelief as the man of her dreams opened his front door and they disappeared inside.

"No, no, no!" she hissed. "This isn't fair. This isn't fair at all!"

\

CHAPTER THIRTY-FIVE

As Cooper had headed off to Ruby's boarding house, Charlie had noticed Hannah directly across the street. He was about to walk up and say hello when she'd hurried after the sheriff. Charlie immediately realized she was following him!

He was torn.

Did he pursue Hannah and find out what she was up to, or go to McTavish's as the sheriff had asked? Then he saw Jimmy Williams. It was widely believed the ten-year-old boy would be President one day. He was frighteningly smart, oddly serious, and responsible far beyond his years.

"Jimmy, come here, quick."

"Hi, Charlie," the boy said, running up to him. "Do you need me?"

"Here's a penny. Run to McTavish's and ask for Patrick Doyle, the man with the red hair. Can you remember that?"

"Patrick Doyle, red hair. What message should I give him?"

"Tell him the bad man has been locked up."

"Why is it called red hair? It's not red, it's orange."

"Dang, you're right," Charlie chuckled, glancing up to see where Hannah was. "I'll think about that. Go on now, and hurry."

As the young lad began sprinting down the street, Charlie turned his attention back to Hannah. She was almost at the end of the block, and the sheriff was turning the corner. Though she suddenly stopped, Charlie could see was continuing to watch.

He broke into a jog, but as he drew near he began to amble, then paused and leaned against the side of a building. When the sheriff reappeared a minute later with Violet at his side, Charlie saw Hannah turn her back to them, but as they started down the street where the sheriff lived, she continued her pursuit.

Charlie had seen enough.

* * *

Hannah was filled with a jealous rage and her head was spinning.

Who was the beautiful girl?

Where had she come from?

Why was she going into Cooper's home?

Then she abruptly remembered the man in the saloon yelling something about a fifty-dollar reward for finding a red-headed woman.

Fifty-dollars was a fortune.

Could it be the pretty lady on Cooper's arm?

She was new in town.

The woman the man wanted had to be her!

"I'm going to sneak into the sheriff's office and ask him," she muttered as she started back down Main Street. "He was really drunk though. I wonder how long it will take him to be normal again."

Her eyes were focused on the dirt road beneath her feet, and she didn't notice the brick wall named Charlie Johnson blocking her path.

She saw his boots too late.

Slamming into him she let out a squeal and staggered backwards, but Charlie caught her arm just as she was about to fall.

"You might wanna watch where you're goin," he scolded as her panicked eyes looked up at him. "Just what are you up to, Hannah Thomas?"

"I don't know what you mean," she retorted. "You're the one who ran into me!"

"We both know that's not true. You followed the sheriff, and you were so busy thinkin' you weren't payin' attention. Now you'd better start talkin."

But she didn't.

She just glared back at him.

"Hannah! Are you listenin'?"

"Of course I'm listening," she snapped. "Why are you yelling at me?"

"I'm not yellin', I'm demandin'. There's a difference. You followed the sheriff. Why?"

"What will you do? Lock me up if I don't tell you?"

"I sure will."

"Fine, then please do," she exclaimed.

Charlie's eyes narrowed.

The girl was scheming.

She wanted to be in the jailhouse, but why?

Suddenly flashing back to the moment he'd run past her on his way to get the handcuffs, it dawned on him. She'd heard Connelly shouting about the reward.

She was going to betray the sheriff!

"What, Charlie? Why are you looking at me like that?"

"You are a wicked, wicked, girl," he replied, his voice low and threatening. "Do you have any idea who that man is?"

"What man? I don't know what you're talking about."

"Don't you play dumb with me," he scolded, watching a pink blush cross her cheeks. "You followed the sheriff to see where he was takin' Violet Parker so you could tell that man sittin' in the jail. Is it the money? You'd let an innocent woman be ripped to shreds for money? Shame on you, Hannah Thomas. Shame on you!"

"What? No, wait," she said urgently. "What do you mean ripped to shreds?"

"He's a monster. He's done terrible things. How about I put you in the same cell with him if you wanna talk to him so bad."

"NO!"

"Then tell me what's goin' on!"

"Please, Charlie, I didn't realize. I swear."

"Dang, it, Hannah! I won't ask again!"

"I was angry because I, uh..."

"Because what? You'd better tell me or so help me I'll do what the sheriff does to misbehavin' females—then I'll put you in that cell."

"What do you mean, what the sheriff does?"

"I'll turn you over my knee and spank your backside, that's what I mean!"

* * *

A funny feeling had been rolling through Hannah's stomach. Hearing the threat, heat surged through her body and she thought she might faint. But out of nowhere, the craziest notion popped into her head. She wanted Charlie Johnson to kiss her!

"Hannah?"

"I thought I..."

"You thought what?" he demanded. "That you'd like fifty dollars?"

"No, no, that's not what I'm talking about. Please, Charlie, don't be mad at me. I was being stupid and jealous and I wasn't thinking straight."

* * *

She was staring up at him with an odd look in her eye, and he realized she was about the prettiest girl he'd ever seen. Her blue eyes were unusually light, the sun was shimmering off her light brown hair making it appear almost golden.

A gush of energy suddenly surged through his loins.

"You and I are gonna have a serious talk," he managed, wishing he could press his lips against her full pink mouth. "Come back to the office with me and we'll sit on the porch."

"Yes, I'd like that, and I would never betray the sheriff, I swear it."

"Seems like that's what you were fixin' to do," he said gruffly, trying to make sense of what was happening.

"I lost my head for a minute, that's all. And it wasn't about the fifty dollars."

"Then you're gonna tell me what it was about," he said firmly, gripping her elbow. "Are we clear about that?"

"Yes, Charlie, and I will try to explain, though I'm not sure I understand it myself. I feel quite differently now. No, that's not true. I feel very differently now."

"Funny thing," he said, suppressing a grin. "So do I."

CHAPTER THIRTY-SIX

While Charlie had been confronting Hannah, Cooper and Violet and entered his home, closed the door, and let out a collective sigh of relief. Smiling at her, he'd wordlessly carried her bag into the second bedroom, placed it on the narrow bed, then brought her into his arms. Closing his eyes, he'd inhaled her sweet fragrance, and when they finally broke apart, he placed his finger under her chin, tilted up her head and locked her eyes.

"I can't tell you how happy I am that you're gonna be stayin' here tonight."

"You don't want me sleeping in here, do you?" she asked with a sassy grin.

"Not for a minute. I just thought you might like your own dressin' room, though it's not much of one."

"Cooper, what a sweet thought," she said softly, and moving her hands to the back of his head, she pressed her lips against his in a long, passionate kiss.

"I really wish you hadn't done that," he said huskily. "I've gotta ride back to the Johnson ranch, and now it's the last thing I wanna do."

"Must you go?"

"I'm afraid so. Zeke has to know about the viper he had under his roof. When I tell him Connelly was arrested and thrown in a cell, his wife won't let him back in."

"Is she a tough lady?"

"She can be. I got the feelin' she didn't like that man from the get-go and she'll be happy to hear the news. I'm not sure about Zeke though.

That man only does favors if he's gettin' a return, and it won't be happenin' this time. But there's another reason I've gotta get over there. Zeke heard some real bad things about you, and I need to set the record straight before rumors start up."

"Oh, my goodness, yes you do. I'd hate the people here to think badly of me."

"Don't worry. I'm gonna make sure Zeke and Millicent get it through their heads you're no murderess."

"It will be such a relief knowing I don't have to worry about that awful detective anymore. Are you sure he'll be leaving in the morning?"

"As sure as I can be, but you're to stay in this house until I know he's gone."

"Then what?"

"I've been thinkin' on that, and we can talk about it more over dinner. Right now I've gotta take off, but before I go, you and I are gonna have a quick talk," he said releasing her and sitting her on the edge of the bed.

"Is it serious?"

"Not like you think, but yeah. What you did at Ruby's, comin' down the stairs and yellin' at the sergeant—"

"But I had to," she said hastily, cutting him off. "You know that, and it was a good thing that I did."

"Uh-huh."

"Why are you looking at me that way?"

"Why do you think, darlin'?"

"You disapprove."

"I sure do, but why?"

"Why don't you just tell me?"

"It's better you think it through."

"Oh, for pity's sake," she grumbled. "Fine. You told me to stay in my room and I didn't listen. There."

"Did you know Doyle? What kinda man he is?"

"No, not really."

"What if he'd been carryin' a gun and decided you were a threat?"

"Uh, I'm not sure."

"What about me? What would I have done?"

"Pulled yours I suppose."

"Then what?"

"Cooper, please stop. I know I should've done as you said, but it all worked out."

"That's beside the point. It could've easily gone the other way. If you'd known Doyle is a peace-lovin' kinda fella that's one thing, but you didn't. You're a risk-taker. I am too, but what you did was downright dangerous for everyone, and you know it. You knew it at the time."

"You're scolding me."

"I sure am, and tonight I'm gonna spank you."

"What?"

"Suddenly the girl who wanted to be spanked doesn't anymore?" he remarked, raising one wicked eyebrow.

"It feels different."

"It is different."

"You won't hurt me, will you?"

"I'd never hurt you, darlin', but I'm sure gonna make your bottom sting."

"You don't have to," she said softly, staring up at him with woeful eyes. "I really am sorry, honest."

"You think that's gonna work?"

"It was worth a try," she muttered, her voice dropping as she let out a resigned sigh.

"You would've been disappointed if I'd given in to that little act, and you know that too."

"Who are you Cooper Dalton?"

"I'm the flip side of you, Violent Parker, and that's why we're such a perfect pair," he said softly. "I'm takin' off now, and you can think about what's gonna happen when I get back."

The butterflies that had been fluttering around her stomach abruptly gave birth to several hundred more, and as she stood up to say goodbye, she impulsively threw her arms around his neck.

"I do love you, Cooper, so very much. You're saving my life."

"You know what," he murmured, moving his lips to her ear, "you're savin' mine too."

CHAPTER THIRTY-SEVEN

Cooper was cantering across the last open field on his way home. It had been an easy meeting with Zeke, but Cooper wasn't surprised. The successful rancher was a pragmatic man. Cooper was the law in Brownsville, well-liked, deeply respected, and kept peace in the town. When he'd told Zeke the detective who'd been staying at the ranch was a viper, and his allegations against Violet Parker were baseless, though Cooper had seen a flash of disappointment, Zeke had simply nodded. Millicent had sighed, then made it clear she'd been suspicious of the Connelly from the start. As Cooper was leaving, he saw one of her sons carrying Connelly's bag out of the house.

"Sheriff, it'll be at the gate. He can pick it up on his way out of town," she'd declared. "Make sure you tell him not to come knocking on my door."

Nearing the outskirts of town, Cooper glanced up at the sky. It was the time of the year for spontaneous storms and he could see dark clouds gathering. As he slowed River to a trot and entered Main Street, a chilly wind swirled around him, giving credence to his suspicions. Approaching his office he saw Charlie sitting on the porch with his head in a book, but the young man looked up and waved. Cooper waved back, and riding around to the back of the building, he climbed off and led River into the corral. After cleaning him up and throwing him some hay, he returned to his office, but as he walked up to Charlie, he thought the young man looked particularly bright.

"Anything goin' on?"

"A bit," Charlie replied. "How did it go with pa?"

"No problems, and your ma had Connelly's bag left by the gate. You said you had some news?"

"Yep, but do you want some coffee? I just made a pot the way you like it. I figured you'd be back around now."

"Sure. I'll wait for you out here."

Settling into a chair, Cooper kicked over the old wooden crate he used as a footstool and wearily put his feet up. A moment later Charlie reappeared carrying two mugs. Cooper gratefully accepted the hot drink.

"Damn, that's good," he said with a satisfied sigh. "Just what I needed."

"What I have to tell you is about Hannah. It's under control now, but I think you should know."

"Go on."

"She followed you when you left earlier. She saw you and Violet go into your house."

"Dang it. She's had a crush on me for a while. I'll have a talk with her and make sure she doesn't start spreadin' rumors. I don't care, but I don't want folks around here thinkin' badly of Violet."

"It was a bit more than nosiness, Sheriff. I confronted her and made her tell me what she was up to. She was plannin' to tell Connelly where Violet was."

"Say, what?" Cooper exclaimed, almost spilling his coffee. "What's gotten into that girl?"

"You don't have to worry. I stopped her right quick."

"Why the blazes would she do somethin' like that?"

"She was jealous, but I scolded her real good, and told her she's not to say a word to anyone."

"Thanks, Charlie. Sounds like you handled her just right."

"I had to send Jimmy Williams off to McTavish's to deliver your message though. It was either follow her, or go over there. I thought it was better to follow her."

"That kid is as reliable as the sun comin' up in the mornin'. Good work, Charlie!"

"Uh, the thing of it is, about Hannah, I'll be callin' on her. We sorta hit it off. I got the feelin' she liked me puttin' her in her place."

"Good for you! Some women like a fella to take a stand. Sounds like she's made that way. It'll make life a whole lot easier."

"She's some spitfire."

"Yep. You'll have your hands full," Cooper remarked with a grin.

"I sure hope so!"

Cooper laughed out loud, then finishing his coffee he stood up and stretched his arms above his head.

"I don't know much about women, Charlie, I'm not sure any man does, but if you ever wanna talk about things I'll be here."

"Thanks, Sheriff. I'll probably be takin' you up on that."

"I'm goin' on home. It's been a long day. Have a good night and I'll see you in the mornin'."

"Night, Sheriff."

As he ambled down the street he put his hands on his hips and chuckled.

"Charlie and Hannah Thomas. How about that?" he muttered. "I can see them makin' a couple. That's real nice."

But as he continued on, his mind turned to Violet.

He could imagine her sitting on the couch wondering how hard he was going to spank her. He frowned. What she'd done wasn't acceptable and he would redden her backside, but he'd make it short and sharp. She'd been a free spirit her entire life and he didn't want to clip her wings, he just wanted her to think about things before acting.

He was surprised to find his door unlocked, but as he walked in he came to an abrupt stop and stared around the room.

It was sparkling clean, and the couch had been moved to face the fireplace, but that wasn't the only change. A low table that had been sitting against the wall serving no purpose, had been placed in front of it, and he realized that's where it should have been all along. Then he noticed the white curtains from the back bedroom had replaced the dark brown ones. He was amazed at how much brighter they made the place. Wild flowers sat on the side table next to the couch, knick-knacks that had been gathering dust in a box in the hall closet were now spread around the room, and the smell of baking filled the air.

His house had been transformed into a home.

CHAPTER THIRTY-EIGHT

Peeking through a crack in the door of her dressing room, and seeing the look of astonishment—then happiness— cross Cooper's face, she dared to step forward.

"What do you think?" She asked tentatively. "I wasn't sure...

"I'm speechless, darlin'. It's, it's, it's fantastic is what it is. I can't believe you did all this."

"I thought it needed a bit of sprucing up and I had nothing better to do. I messed with the bedroom a bit as well."

"Let me see!"

Striding forward and taking her hand, he marched down the short hall, and caught his breath as he entered.

She'd changed the angle of the bed, and it seemed to double the size of the room. The grey bedspread was gone, and in its place was a cream blanket he kept as a spare in the closet. Staring at it he realized just how drab the old coverlet had been. She'd also moved in the oval mirror from the back bedroom and placed it in a corner. The transformation was remarkable. The room had gone from drab and dreary to warm and inviting.

"I'd like to get you a new bedspread, but I think that looks nice for the moment."

"I cannot believe what you've done. I swear I don't know what to say. Thank you, Violet, and what's that smell?"

"I made us some apple cinnamon pie."

"How? I had nothin' in the house."

"Yes you did. In the little pantry you had flour and some eggs, and a small packet of cinnamon. Didn't you know that? I picked the apples from the tree in the backyard."

"Dang. That's right! Someone brought it over at Christmas."

"I'd better check on it. I don't know how hot your oven gets."

"Where did you learn to cook?"

"Life," she said with a wink. "My room didn't have an oven, but I'd use one of the kitchens in the neighborhood to make treats for the children. I also spent some time with Earl's cook. She was a lovely lady."

"What a shame," he said, following her through to the kitchen.

"What's that?"

"You've done such a wonderful thing, and I have to spank you."

She paused her step, and turning around she tilted her head to the side. "But of course you do. The two things are separate. I didn't do all this to try to wheedle out of being punished. I did it because I wanted to do something special for you. Something to say thank you for everything you've done for me. I was going to buy you a present but I couldn't leave the house, and then it occurred to me I could do something even better."

"You, Violet Parker," he said softly, moving up to her and taking her into his arms, "are special, real special. Your heart is so dang big, and even after goin' through so much, you're so—so—I can't find the word. Grace. That's what you have—grace."

Leaning in, he began drifting his lips over hers, then softly sucked in her lower lip, and as he gently broke away, he gazed into her sparkling green eyes.

"You're gonna think I'm crazy and I probably am, but sometimes..."

"Sometimes what?" she asked, a strange feeling moving through her. "Why are you looking at me like that?"

"Marry me— tomorrow—just the two of us. No big fancy weddin'. Charlie can stand up for me, and Ruby can stand up for you. Whatta ya say?"

"But we've only—"

"If you're gonna say we've only just met, don't bother. You know we're meant for each other, and you know how quick life can be snatched away. If Earl hadn't taken so long to ask you to marry him..."

"I've thought about that more often than you can imagine," she murmured. "I think he only waited to pacify his daughter."

"Violet, meetin' each other is a blessin', and I don't wanna miss a single day bein' with you. Come on, darlin'! You've always taken chances. Do it again. Take my hand and let's jump off the cliff together. I swear I'll break your fall."

"Yes! Yes! Yes! Yes! Yes!" she suddenly exclaimed, throwing her arms around his neck and hugging him tightly, then she suddenly pulled back and stared at him with a worried frown. "What will we do about rings?"

"Good question," he said with a knowing smile. "When my pa died, my mother took his weddin' band, and told me when she passed I should take hers too. She was worried about grave robbers."

"Grave robbers?"

"Folks who dig up graves to steal what the dead are buried with."

"That's horrible."

"She didn't want those precious pieces of gold that meant so much to her, endin' up in the hands of thieves."

"Cooper. That makes me sad and happy at the same time."

"Yeah, me too."

"So, uh, are we really going to do this?" she whispered, gazing up at him.

"Yep, Violet, you bet, except..."

"What?"

"I just remembered. The preacher's gonna be buryin' old man Flint in the afternoon, so I reckon it'll have to be in the mornin'."

"Oh, my goodness," she said with a giggle, "My mother is probably laughing in heaven about all this, but my poor father will be horrified. I remember him being very proper."

"I expect he's pleased you found someone to keep you in line," Cooper said with a wink. "You haven't told me much about your folks, and I want to hear all about them."

"I'll tell you, of course I will, but if we're doing this in the morning, don't we need to see Ruby and let her know?"

"Yep, I reckon we do, but we've got some unfinished business. There's no better way to start our lives together than with a good spankin'. Go into the bedroom, pull up that dress, pull down your drawers, and bend over the bed. I'll be in shortly."

As her tummy tumbled, and she felt the familiar heat flame across her face, she stared at him wondering why God was blessing her so richly after all her misdeeds.

"I love you Cooper Dalton," she said softly, then fervently kissing him, she turned and hurried away.

* * *

Standing alone in his kitchen, he remembered how he used to feel when he'd see his mother so sad.

For the first time he understood.

He was a risk-taker, but loving Violet and marrying her was the biggest risk of his life.

CHAPTER THIRTY-NINE

Stretched over the bed and waiting for Cooper, Violet didn't know if her heart was pounding from his unexpected proposal, or the spanking she was about to receive, then decided it was probably both. Suddenly hearing him enter, she took a deep breath to settle her nerves, but when she looked over her shoulder she found he was carrying a wooden spoon.

"Not your hand?"

"Not this time. It'll be quick and it'll sting. It'll be both a punishment and a warnin'. I'm not gonna spank you real hard cos I know you were driven to say your piece, but you've gotta learn to do as I ask. I'm the sheriff in this town. If people see my wife doin' whatever she pleases it's not gonna go down well for either of us."

"Your wife," she repeated, smiling in spite of her ungainly position.

"Yep," he said, grinning back. "Are you ready?"

"No...yes."

Moving forward and sitting on the edge of the bed, he began smoothing the makeshift paddle across her naked cheeks.

"I'll ask again. Are you ready?"

"If you insist."

"Say, what?"

"Sorry. Sometimes I can't help myself."

"That's the sassy girl in you, and I'm takin' it as a yes."

She felt him lightly tapping the hard spoon against her skin, it only lasted a short time before he landed hard swats every few seconds.

"Ow! Those hurt."

"You mean like this?" he asked, landing more.

"Ooh, yes, please will you be done soon?"

"Ask me again and it will last longer. I'll be done when I'm done. If you don't listen, you get spanked. It's not difficult. Now hush up."

Burying her face in the soft blanket, though the swats grew harder and sting increased, she began to experience an unfamiliar sense of satisfaction...and felt a warm flood between her legs. When his fingers unexpectedly slipped between her legs, she arched her back and wriggled lewdly.

"Whatta you beggin' for?" he asked huskily. "You want me inside you?"

"Yes, please, so much."

"Are you listenin'?"

"Yes, Sir."

"Next time you do somethin' reckless I'll bring out the spoon, but I'll leave you like wantin' me like this. You understand?"

"I understand, and that would be worse than the spanking."

"Yep. Remember that. No puttin' yourself in danger. Those days are over."

* * *

Violet's pussy was glistening with its slick wetness, and Cooper was aching to slide inside her. Dropping his trousers, he placed himself at her entrance and slowly thrust forward, relishing the feel of her drenched channel. Delighting in the sight of her red backside, he grabbed her hips, slowly withdrew, then plunged back in. She let out a wail, but he repeated the slow, ardent attack, continuing until she was begging him to move faster. He was happy to oblige, and pummeling her pussy he brought her to the brink, then to the mewling of her frustration and disappointment, he pulled out.

"Why did you stop?"

"Climb on the bed and take off the rest of your clothes."

He stripped as he watched her, then laying on top of her naked body, he reached underneath her and cupped her hot cheeks, eliciting a loud yelp.

"Are you complainin'?"

"A bit," she mumbled, "but not really."

"You wanna come, darlin'?"

"Yes, yes, so much."

Stroking with a steady rhythm, he focused on her responses, accelerating then slowing each time she was about to climax.

"Please, Cooper," she finally panted, "I can't stand it another minute. Please won't you let me have my orgasm?"

He answered by moving his lips to her nipples, and staying buried inside her, he sucked each in turn, taking his time as she wriggled beneath him until his cock was aching to explode.

"Are you gonna be a good girl?" he purred, traveling his mouth to her neck.

"Yes, I swear," she bleated. "Please...."

"The Sheriff giveth, and the sheriff can withhold. Will you remember that when you're my wife?"

"I will, I promise."

"If you throw a tantrum you know what could happen," he warned, his voice a hot whisper as he began to pump, "but I've got other bullets in my gun. Anytime you wanna find out what they are, you just let me know and I'll be happy to give you a taste."

"Please, I'm there, I'm there..." she wailed, his words sending her over the edge. "Please..."

Pressing his mouth on hers with a crushing kiss, he muffled her euphoric wails, and a moment later it cloaked his own deep groans.

* * *

The sun was low in the sky when they set off to speak to the preacher. The church was just outside of town near McTavish's Boarding House.

If they were able to arrange the ceremony, they'd stop in and see Ruby and Charlie on their way back, but as they passed Al's Mercantile they found him closing up for the day. Violet tugged at Cooper's arm and asked him to stop.

"Please, I want him at the wedding," Violet said in a hushed whisper. "He's been so kind to me."

"Then let's ask him, and you can officially introduce yourself. He still thinks you're Rose Hamilton."

Al was overjoyed with the news, surprised to hear Rose's name was actually Violet, and upset that she'd had to hide out because of a crooked detective.

"Sheriff, I gotta say, I never thought I'd see you get hitched," he remarked with a grin. "It'll be a real honor for the missus and me to be there."

"I never thought I would be either, but I can't wait," Cooper replied, smiling along with him. "I just hope the preacher doesn't have anything else to do."

"If he does I reckon he'll be happy to put it off. What time?"

"Ten o'clock, but if that changes I'll come by in the mornin' and let you know, and Al, keep it under your hat. We just want a quiet affair."

"Sure thing, but my wife will have a hard time. She'll want to tell everyone."

"Then don't let her into the secret until the last minute," Violet suggested, "and I think we'd better get to the church, don't you, Cooper? That sun is setting fast!"

"Yep, I agree. Bye, Al, and thanks."

"I couldn't be happier," Al beamed. "See you in the mornin'."

They continued on, but a moment later they were interrupted by the clerk from the telegraph office.

"Sheriff, I was just on my way to see you. I've got some telegrams here. Two for you, and one for a man named Detective Connelly. Isn't that the fella you've got locked up?"

"Sure is. Thanks, Jeremiah. I'll make sure he gets it."

"Do you know who the telegrams are from?" Violet asked as they continued walking and he ripped open the first.

"This one's from the sheriff in Peabody. He's sending his deputies over tomorrow to pick up our rustler turned bank robber, and this one," he continued, opening the second, "I'm hopin' is gonna make you real happy. Yep. This is about the best weddin' present you could get."

"What?"

"I'll tell you as we walk, but get ready for a surprise."

CHAPTER FORTY

Inside the Sheriff's office Charlie was finishing up a hearty meal. His mother had been missing her youngest son, and worried he wasn't eating properly she'd sent George into town with a care package. Charlie had found himself with enough food to last him several days, including a freshly baked cake. It had been a wonderful surprise, and as he wiped his dish clean with a piece of bread and popped it in his mouth, he let out a contented sigh.

Life was good.

He loved his new job, he was much happier living away from his annoying older brothers, and he was totally smitten with Hannah.

Packing away the plate, he made sure everything was sealed so it wouldn't attract the vile vermin, then fetching the broom he swept out the office and carried it into the back to clean around the cells.

"How long am I gonna be in here," the foiled bank robber asked as Charlie worked.

"Not sure, but I'm guessin' the deputies from Peabody will be here tomorrow afternoon. At least you have some company now."

"Company? You call that company?"

Connelly had left his cot and was sprawled out on the floor. With his lanky arms and legs wide apart he covered almost the entire area.

"Better than a rat," Charlie muttered. "Are you finished with your bowl?"

"Yeah, thanks. It was pretty good. The saloon must have the women cookin'."

Leaning the broom against the wall, Charle collected the bowls and carried them out to the office just as Cooper and Violet walked in.

"This is a surprise. Isn't it a bit chilly out there for a sunset walk?"

"Yep, so we can't stay long, but we have some news. I'll tell you the borin' part first. A deputy will be here to pick up our rustler—bank robber tomorrow afternoon."

"I'll tell him. He was just askin' about that."

"Are you busy at around ten in the mornin'?"

"Uh, no, but I'm thinkin' maybe I will be," he replied with a grin. "What's happenin'?"

"How would you like to stand up for me at my weddin'? Violet and I are gettin' married."

"Are you jokin'?" he exclaimed, totally stunned by the unexpected news. "Heck yeah, I'm honored, real honored, and, uh, hey, I've got a cake. You need a cake? Ma sent it over. I want you to have it. Who else is comin'? Dang."

"Thank you, Charlie," Violet giggled, delighted by his enthusiastic reaction. "We'd love to share your cake."

"I'll ride to the ranch first thing to get my good clothes. No! I'll ride over there now. I'll have just enough time before it gets dark."

"You might as well pick up Connelly's bag and bring it back with you. I think your ma would appreciate that."

"I sure will, and thanks again, Sheriff."

"You've more than proven yourself over these last few days, Charlie, and you'll be my deputy real soon. We're a team now."

"Really? Wow, that's great, Sheriff. Thanks."

"We'll talk about it later. Right now we have to see Mrs. Elwood. Make sure you lock up when you take off."

"Sure will, Sheriff. See you in the mornin'. Dang! I can't believe it!"

* * *

A short time later, sitting in the parlor at Ruby's, Violet shared the joyous news. Ruby was just as excited as Charlie, but after hugging them both she nodded her head knowingly.

"Sheriff, the day you brought this lovely young lady to my door, I knew the two of you were meant for each other. You looked like a couple even then. Now, let's see, I'll bake you a cake, and we'll come back here for a celebration lunch."

"Millicent Johnson baked a cake for Charlie and he wants us to have it, so I think the cake is taken care of," Cooper said, "but I sure appreciate the offer. "

"Then I'll make a meat pie and some other things. You can't have a wedding without a party, even if it's a small one. You say Al and his wife are coming, and Charlie too? Anyone else?"

"You know, I just had a thought," Cooper declared. "We need some good wine. I'm runnin' over to the saloon. I'll arrange for it to be delivered here first thing. Is that all right with you, Ruby?"

"Of course."

"I'll be real quick," he promised, and pecking Violet on the cheek, he hurried away.

"Now, Violet," Ruby began with a happy smile, "I'd like to come over in the morning and help you get ready."

"That would be wonderful. Thank you. The dress I'm wearing needs a corset and I can't handle that alone."

"I've got quite a talent for styling hair as well, and yours is so beautiful I simply have to fix it for you."

"Thank you, I would love that."

"Tell me, have you had a chance to tell the Sheriff about your parents?"

"I plan to when we get home."

"I've been thinking. It's possible your father's family has no idea he's passed away. Maybe they think his silence is deliberate. Time has a way of healing wounds. In any event, you should think about tracking them down. It's unlikely they'll hold a grudge against you, and you have a right to know your history."

"Where would I even start?"

"The sheriff will probably be able to help. He's been out in the world and he knows more than most. He was once a professional gunslinger."

"Yes, he told me."

"It was said he could draw faster than the eye could see."

"He's never without that holster."

"He's the Sheriff, he has to wear it, but you should ask him to show you how he can shoot."

The sound of the front door interrupted their conversation, and a moment later Cooper walked in wearing an odd expression.

"What?"

"Um, well, I'm not sure how to tell you this," he said sheepishly. "I whispered to Josie why I needed the wine, but I guess I wasn't quiet enough. One of the other girls heard me. She stood up on a table and announced our weddin' to the entire saloon. They've promised to stay away from the church, but they're spreadin' the word and plannin' a big party for tomorrow night. Sorry."

"Why are you sorry? That's wonderful. I can't wait to meet everyone."

"I've been wantin' to cook you a special dinner since you arrived," Ruby declared. "Come here first, then go over. I might even join you for a little while."

"That's too much trouble," Violet protested. "A celebration in the morning and dinner in the evening."

"If you're lucky you only get married once, and I'm tickled that I can contribute to your special day. I'm not going to take no for an answer."

"Looks like it's gonna be a heck of a weddin' day," Cooper said with a grin. "As long as I end the day at home with my new bride, that's all I care about."

CHAPTER FORTY-ONE

In spite of the pending nuptials, Violet and Cooper slept better than they had in a very long time. After years of fearing the evil detective, Violet could breathe again, and Cooper had not only seen his house become a warm, comfortable home, he'd found in Violet something he never thought he'd have. A woman he loved. When they woke in the morning, though he was aching to take her into his arms, he felt the need to wait until after their wedding. To his delight and surprise Violet had the same inkling.

"I don't know why it should matter," she said as she snuggled against him, "but it does."

"Yeah, it's a strange thing. I guess it's the way the Good Lord wants it to be, but I'm not sorry we've been together."

"Oh, my goodness, neither am I," she said vehemently. "I'll never forget that time at Ruby's. Do you think she knew?"

"I don't think she misses much, but it's hard to say."

"She's such a lovely lady."

"Yep, and speakin' of lovely ladies, are you about ready to get hitched?"

"So ready and so happy."

"Then we'd better get outta this bed."

"Yes, we'd better. Ruby will be here shortly. I hung my dress up last night, so the wrinkles should be out."

"A special dress?"

"It's never been worn. Earl bought it for me. We were supposed to be attending a dinner party, and I didn't have the heart to leave it behind. I know he'll be looking down on us and giving us his blessing."

"You'd look beautiful wearin' a sack."

"I don't think so."

"I do, and I'm not sure I can hold out much longer so I'm gettin' up. You feel so good it should be against the law."

* * *

Though Violet and Cooper were deliriously happy, the same couldn't be said for Detective Frank Connelly. Waking up in the cell on the cold hard floor, his head pounding and every muscle in his body aching, he tried to remember how he'd ended up there. His last recall was drinking with the sheriff, arguing, then the world spinning so fast he'd toppled over.

"You're finally awake."

Slowly sitting up, he turned his head and saw an unkempt cowboy in the adjacent cell.

"Yeah. What's it to you?"

"Just bein' neighborly."

"I'm not in the mood," Frank snarled, reaching out to the cot for support as he staggered to his feet. But as he did he spied a folded piece of paper with his name scrawled across it. "What the fuck is that?"

"The kid brought it in last night."

Still on his knees, Frank picked it up, and with bleary eyes he read the short sharp telegram.

RETURN IMMEDIATELY. CAPTAIN GRAYSON

Blind fury coursed through his veins.

"Goddamned Doyle," he grunted, then frowned from both a sharp stabbing pain in his head, and an unexpected moment of clarity. "No, Doyle wouldn't dare cross me. The sheriff. I'll bet that goddamned Violet Parker sold him some tale. I'll kill them both."

"Not this mornin' you won't," his fellow prisoner declared.

"Obviously! I'm locked up in this fucking cell!"

"You sure cuss a lot."

"Like I said before, what's it to you."

"I wasn't talkin' about you bein' stuck in here."

"Then what?"

"The sheriff's gettin' married. I heard them talkin' last night. That Violet Parker you just mentioned, that's his bride."

"I knew it," Frank hissed. "She spun her web and that idiot sheriff walked right into it. Where? Tell me where?"

"They said at the church, and as far as I know there's only one. It's just past a boardin' house on that first lane as you leave town. You know, you don't look too good."

"I feel fucking worse."

"The kid will be bringin' us a cuppa coffee any minute now. That'll help."

"The only thing that will help me is grabbing that she-devil and hauling her ass out of this hellhole, and believe me that's exactly what I'll do!"

* * *

Ruby stared in absolute awe as Violet stood in front of her. The dress was the most exquisite gown she'd ever seen. Cream lace from the hem to the high collar was layered over shiny satin, a band at the waist accentuated Violet's svelte figure, and pearl buttons traveled up the center of the bodice, flattering her porcelain complexion. After Ruby had curled Violet's hair around her head with hairpins, Violet had produced a tortoiseshell comb with pearls across the edge. Set off to the side, it was the perfect compliment for both the hairstyle and the elegant dress.

"I swear, I've never seen a woman look more beautiful," Ruby murmured, feeling the threat of happy tears.

"There's one more thing I want to wear," Violet said, opening her bag and withdrawing the diamond watch.

"Land sakes."

"I might not be here today if it hadn't been for the man who gave this to me. He restored my faith in people. I want to wear it in memory of him. I didn't love him the way I love Cooper, but I'll always cherish him. I know he's looking down from heaven overjoyed that I've found happiness."

"That's mighty sweet, and I'll just bet he is."

CHAPTER FORTY-TWO

Cooper, dressed in his fine suit, had been waiting anxiously in the living room. When Violet walked in, he felt a wave of emotion so deep he almost staggered.

"You—you—you are a vision," he breathed. "An angel sent from heaven. What have I done to deserve this?"

"Cooper, stop, you'll make me weep."

"Why?"

"The way you're looking at me. No-one has ever looked at me like that."

"That's because..." he said softly, walking up to her and gazing into her emerald green eyes, "no-one could ever love you as much as I do."

"I don't deserve someone so honest and good."

"Darlin', I wasn't always, remember? You deserve every stitch of happiness I can offer, and I'll do my best to put a smile on your face every day."

But a knock broke the moment.

"It's me, Al, I'm here with my wagon to take you to the church."

"I'll answer it," Ruby declared, hurrying past them and opening the door. "Oh, my stars!" she exclaimed, stepping back.

"Ruby? What's the matter?" Cooper asked, taking Violet's hand and walking quickly across the room.

"Howdy, Sheriff," Al said, stepping inside to greet him. "The wife and I got to thinkin', and, well...this is our weddin' gift."

Moving aside, he waved his arm, and as they walked outside, they found Al's wagon covered with pink ribbons and garlands of flowers.

"It's just perfect!" Violet exclaimed. "Al, how wonderful. Thank you."

"I'm glad you like it," he said with a wide smile.

As the happy group settled into the gaily adorned wagon, the shop-keeper drove his horse forward, but when they turned at the end of the block, both sides of Main Street were lined with people.

"What did you say about a quiet wedding?" Violet laughed as they passed the cheering townsfolk.

"I never expected anything like this," he muttered, amazed by the crowd. "This is unbelievable."

"You deserve it, Sheriff," Ruby declared. "You've made this town a safe and happy place to live."

The wagon continued to roll down Main Street, and reaching the outskirts of the town, they turned into the lane by the trees, passed Mc-Tavish's Boarding House, and finally reached the church.

With Al and Ruby walking ahead of them, Violet and Cooper moved up the path and through the heavy oak doors. Entering the church and seeing the waiting preacher, and Charlie ready to stand up for Cooper, Violet thought her heart would burst from joy. But glancing up at him, she saw a worried frown crossing his forehead.

"Cooper? Is something wrong?"

"Not a thing darlin', I just felt a chill," he said softly. "Must be the damp in the air."

But Cooper had lied.

Something was telling him to stay alert, and as they reached the altar, while Violet was speaking with the preacher, Cooper took Charlie aside.

"Connelly is still locked up, right? You checked before you left?"

"Sure did, Sheriff. He looked like death. I bet he had one helluva hang-over, and that telegram sure put him outta sorts."

"But he was locked up. You're sure!"

"Yep. I'm sure."

"Gentlemen," the preacher called, "are you ready?"

Cooper wanted to tell himself he was imagining things, but he knew to ignore his instincts was foolish at best, and at worst, it could prove disastrous.

"I sure am," Cooper replied. "I just need a quick word with my beautiful bride and Charlie. I promise it'll only take a second. Violet, Charlie, could you come here for a minute?"

"What is it?" Violet asked as they stepped away from the altar.

"Violet, when I tell you this, I don't want you to react. Just keep smilin'."

"Uh, okay."

"That goes for you too, Charlie."

"Sure, Sheriff."

"I've got a bad feelin'," he said quietly. "I think Connelly might be lurkin'."

"No, don't say that," Violet whispered.

"Keep smilin' darlin'," Cooper said quickly. "I could be wrong, but we've gotta be ready just in case. Charlie, if anything happens, you protect Violet. Don't worry about Connelly. I'll handle him. Your job will be to get her outta here."

"Sure, Sheriff."

"Violet? Are you okay?"

"I'm fine, and if anything does happen I won't panic," she said confidently, then taking a breath, she added, "but if that devil shows up in God's house on my wedding day, he'll be sorry."

"If he does, leave him to me," Cooper said firmly. "Now let's get wed. I can't wait to call you my wife."

"That's strange" she murmured as they moved back to the altar.

"What's that?" Cooper asked.

"Everything will be fine, but you must stay relaxed. I have no idea why I said that, but, uh, yeah, you need to take a breath."

Her green eyes were blazing into his, and he did as she said, then smiled, and turned to face the preacher.

"Friends, we're gathered in this holy place to witness the joining of these two souls in holy matrimony. If there is anyone here who knows of any reason they should not wed, speak now or forever hold your peace."

"I've got a reason! She's coming back to San Francisco with me," Frank Connelly shouted. *"Turn around Sheriff. I've got a gun aimed at—"*

CHAPTER FORTY-THREE

Cooper had moved with such speed no-one realized he'd spun and drawn his gun until after the shot had been fired. By the time Violet jerked her head around, Connelly was clutching his arm as he tumbled to the floor, and Cooper had holstered his revolver.

"Go cuff him, Charlie," he ordered as he pulled Violet into his arms.

"One minute he was talking, and the next—" Violet said breathlessly. "Cooper, how did you do that?"

"Practice. Ruby, are you all right?"

"I believe I am, Sheriff, though I might have a spot of brandy when we get back to my house."

"Faster than a rattler's strike," Al muttered as he comforted his wife.

"Preacher, what about you?" Cooper asked. "I sure am sorry I had to do that in your church."

"I'm a bit stunned, but yes, I'm fine. I didn't even see you move."

"Neither did he," Cooper muttered gravely, "and it's just as well."

"You got him in the arm," Charlie exclaimed as he hurriedly returned carrying Connelly's pistol. "I don't think it's life-threatenin'."

"That's what I was aimin' for. Glad to see I hit my mark."

"What should I do with him?"

"Take him out to the wagon and make sure he can't get away."

"Sheriff, I swear that cell was locked," Charlie said earnestly.

"I believe you, and don't worry, we'll figure it out. Take care of him and get back in here. It's time for me to get wed."

"Are you saying you want to continue?" the preacher asked. "Surely the wounded man must be seen to."

"I grazed him just enough so he'd drop his gun. A shot through the heart would have been too good for that monster. He'll be fine."

"Violet, what about you," the preacher continued. "Are you still ready to continue?"

"I've never been more ready for anything in my life. I'm marrying my hero."

* * *

Following the short, romantic ceremony, everyone returned to Ruby's house except Charlie. He'd been tasked with fetching the doctor, and making sure Connelly was handcuffed, sedated, and being guarded by Patrick Doyle at McTavish's Boarding House until he could find out how the detective had escaped.

As the small happy group gathered in Ruby's parlor, the conversation moved from the dramatic events in the church to the couple's honeymoon.

"I'll take a few days away once I can arrange for a replacement," Cooper said happily. "For the moment I'd like to spend some time decoratin' my house and makin' it just right for my beautiful bride. You might not see me on the street as much, but I'll be there if I'm needed, and Al, I'll be back and forth to your store quite a bit for curtains and such."

"I never thought I'd hear you say something like that," Al chuckled, "but there's plenty to choose from."

"Is that the front door?" Ruby asked, rising to her feet. "It must be your deputy."

"He's not my deputy yet, but he might as well be," Cooper said proudly. "I'll be swearin' him in real soon."

"Connelly's back in his cell," Charlie exclaimed, walking into the room. "Can you please tell me why you're sendin' him back to the city and not arrestin' him and keepin' him here?"

"I'm happy to, but Charlie, I take it you found out how he escaped."

"Darned if it wasn't those long arms of his. He reached through the bars, got hold of the broom I left against the wall, and was able to get the key off its hook. They're in a drawer in your desk now."

"I'm glad to hear it. Is the other prisoner still there?"

"Yep, but none too happy Connelly didn't help him."

"Okay, Sheriff," Ruby piped up. "It's time to tell us why you're letting that awful man go back to San Francisco."

"I want his victims to see him in prison for what he did to them, not what happened in the church. He hurt women and hard-workin; shop-keepers. They need to see justice done."

"There's very little that would make them happier," Violet murmured. "They'll weep when they hear this, every last one of them."

"But how can you be sure that will happen?" Ruby asked. "Snakes like him have a habit of wriggling out of things."

"What happened today was unexpected, but everything was already set up for his return. You all know I used to be a gunslinger. Henry Coburn, the man who turned my life around, is a State Senator now. I sent him an urgent telegram and he's makin' a special trip to Connelly's station house. When that dirtbag detective gets back, he'll be marched into his office, and in front of the Captain, and hopefully some of his victims, the senator will personally order him to unlock a certain desk drawer. Do you want to tell them what's in it, Violet?"

"Wads of money, probably from the store owners, and the things he's stolen from the women he's attacked."

"Those poor people," Ruby murmured. "Thank goodness he'll be stopped."

"That's just the beginnin'." Cooper continued. "The senator has promised government aid and a jobs program to help the forgotten women and children."

"Cooper, this is just wonderful news," Violet declared with tears in her eyes.

"You and I will go back to visit soon," he promised, lowering his voice. "You can see your friends, and make sure they're gettin' the help they need. Now let's get on with this celebratin'," he exclaimed, turning to face everyone. "I'm hungry and thirsty, and I need to toast my new bride."

CHAPTER FORTY-FOUR

After a few touching speeches, the cake had been cut and the delicious lunch enjoyed. Glancing through a window at the darkening sky, Cooper used the threatening weather as an excuse to leave. He wanted to stroll back to his home with his wife before the rain started. As they stepped outside, and everyone waved them off, he put his arm around her shoulders.

"How are you, Mrs. Dalton?"

"Never better, Mr. Dalton. What about you?"

"Never better, Mrs. Dalton, and as much as I wanna spend the rest of the day naked with you, I love you in that dress. You look like a Princess. I swear you're the most beautiful thing on God's green earth."

"And I thought you were the handsomest man ever the first minute I saw you. Mind you, I haven't seen many half-naked sheriffs," she giggled. "Heavens! I'm so happy, and just a short while ago I was running for my life."

"Life can change mighty fast, there's no doubt about it."

"Cooper, I've been thinking. I do love this watch Earl gave me, but now that I'm able to sell it I think I should."

"So you can give the money to your old neighborhood?"

"Exactly. What do you think?"

"It's up to you, but I think you should hold on to it."

"You do?"

"I was thinkin', maybe you could pass it on to our first daughter."

"Cooper, oh, my goodness, yes. It could become a family heirloom. I'm feeling all emotional again."

They'd reached the house, and as they walked up the path, Cooper swooped her into his arms.

"How are you going to unlock the door?"

"Uh, good question. I think by doin' this," he replied, deftly moving her over his shoulder.

"Cooper Dalton, you'd better not tear my dress!"

"Don't be givin' me any ideas!" he chuckled as he carried her inside, and giving her a swat he added. "I kinda like havin' you up there."

"Would you please put me down?"

"Since you asked so nicely."

Gently placing her on her feet, he took her in his arms and fervently kissed her for endless minutes, leaving them both breathless when they finally broke apart.

"You were amazing in that church," she murmured, resting her head against his chest. "Who knows what that monster would've done if you hadn't shot him."

"You made it possible."

"Me?" she said, pulling back and staring up at him. "I don't understand."

"What you told me when we were goin' back to the altar. You said everything would be okay. Then you said I should take a deep breath and relax. That was a gift. A man can't draw fast and shoot straight if he's tense. A bit wired, sure, that's natural, but not tense. I was wound up about gettin' married, and your words reminded me I needed to settle."

"They came to me like someone had whispered them in my ear."

"Huh, and I have no idea how I knew he was there."

"Maybe an angel is watching over us. Do you believe in angels, Cooper?"

"I sure do. I just married one."

"You can't spank an angel," she softly quipped, twinkling up at him.

"I can if they're earthbound. Would you like remindin'?"

"I'd like to lay in bed with you and have you hold me."

"Darlin', that's about the best idea I ever heard."

* * *

A short time later, as she curled against him and sank into his arms, the anticipated storm boomed to life. With the sound of the rain on the roof, he traversed her body with his lips, and wandered his hands over her curves, until her begging sighs sent him inside her. Locking his fingers into hers, he consumed her mouth as he rode them forward into spine-tingling orgasms.

As they rested together with their limbs entwined, drifting in their euphoric bliss, he heard her mumble.

"Sorry, darlin', what did you say?"

"We have a problem."

"We do?"

"I don't know how to tell you this."

"Just tell me."

"You have to quit. You can't be the sheriff here anymore. It's the only answer."

"Why? Because of the laws you broke to survive? That's in the past."

"No, it's not that," she replied solemnly.

"Then what is it?"

"Because," she said with a dramatic sigh, "you can never leave this bed."

As relief flooded his body he broke into a devilish grin, and rolling on top of her, he pinned her hands on either side of her head.

"You, my darlin' angel, just bought yourself one very red, very hot backside!"

EPILOGUE

Having no idea what was waiting for him, Detective Frank Connelly used the many hours during the coach ride back to San Francisco developing his defense.

He had to create a plausible explanation for arriving at the church, and he was sure arresting a wanted swindler would be enough to get him off the hook. Going against the Captain's orders would result in disciplinary action, but he could handle that. Once things had settled down, he'd return to Brownsville, arrest Violet, and get his horse back.

Walking into the station he was filled with confidence, and though still in handcuffs with Patrick Doyle escorting him, he had no doubt he'd be back on top in no time.

Patrick had been uncharacteristically aggressive during the journey, and Frank had decided the uncomfortable trip had put the sergeant in a bad mood. But it was unacceptable, and Frank would make sure Patrick suffer for his bad attitude.

But as they walked into the Captain's office, Frank knew immediately something was horribly wrong.

A tall, brawny, mature man dressed in a tailored suit, was sitting in front of the Captain's desk. The man was introduced as Senator Henry Coburn, and before Frank could say a word, he marched down the hall to his office. As he opened the door, he was shocked to find a crowd of women and shopkeepers. He recognized them all, and the cold hand of fear clutched his heart.

When the Senator ordered him to unlock the top drawer, Frank's fear turned to panic. As the contents were revealed, and the victims stepped forward and identified their belongings, Frank was arrested and charged on the spot.

Frank knew what would be waiting for him in prison, but even as he desperately tried to think of a way to escape, he knew it would be impossible.

He was done for.

* * *

Patrick was given high praise for his efforts in Brownsville, but he returned home weary and ravenous. His wife drew him a hot bath and cooked his favorite meal. With his body and spirit refreshed, he lounged in his favorite armchair and told her about the peaceful, safe, warm community, and the kind people who lived there. She was receptive, and suggested the family visit and stay for a week. If the children liked it she'd consider the dramatic, life-changing move. Patrick smiled. Open space, horses and dogs. It would be heaven for them. He went to bed that night still tired, but happy and optimistic.

* * *

It took several weeks, and Henry Coburn's personal involvement, but the documents sent to the orphanage with Violet were recovered.

In addition to the family's belongings, her father had left her a substantial amount of money. In the years since she'd fled, the unscrupulous owners had made various attempts to steal it. Fortunately the paperwork her father had put in place was iron-clad. Violet may have been missing, but without proof of her death the funds and property remained untouched.

It was astonishing news, but there was more.

Violet had misunderstood the history of her parent's estrangement from their relatives. It wasn't her father who had been a member of the aristocracy, but her mother.

Margaret Elizabeth Victoria Cheltenham was the first-born daughter of a Duke. She had fallen in love with Albert Jonathan Parker, the man who designed her elegant wardrobe. Though much sought after and highly regarded, he was a commoner, and her family had been outraged. But Margaret and Albert would not be swayed.

Disappearing and boarding a ship for the new world, their elopement had been a huge scandal, but they had been blissfully happy. Shortly after their arrival, Margaret had fallen pregnant, and had given birth to a beautiful baby daughter. They'd named her, Violet Margaret Alberta.

A lawyer named Michael McPherson had traveled to Brownsville to deliver the astounding information. Sitting quietly in their modest home, Cooper and Violet had listened quietly as he had detailed Violet's newfound wealth and noble birth.

"You know I'm at Mrs. Elwood's Boarding House, and I can stay here as long as you need me. I'm sure you'll have some questions."

"Much obliged," Cooper said, walking him to the door, then moving slowly back to Violet waiting on the couch, he sat down and took her hand. "I knew you were a Princess," he said softly. "A beautiful, copper-haired, green-eyed Princess."

Taking a deep breath, she curled her fingers around his.

"I'm your wife," she managed, as unexpected tears spilled down her cheeks, "and you're my husband. That will never change. I know my history now, and it's amazing, but that's all it is, a history."

"Darlin', you can't ignore the fact that I'm just an ex-gunman who's now the sheriff of a small town, and you're an aristocrat and a rich woman."

"I became a rich woman the day I stepped off that stage coach and met you," she said earnestly. "Maybe we could bring some of my belongings here, I'd like that, but the money? Except for setting some aside for emergencies, please let's put it into a fund to help those children I left behind, and others I don't even know. Maybe we can even fix that horrible orphanage."

"What about contactin' your relatives over in England?"

"Why would I want to meet people who turned their backs on my wonderful parents? They're obviously judgmental and...um...now that I think about it..."

"You're changin' your mind?"

"I think perhaps I do want to meet them," she said with a wicked grin. "Yes! I want to go to England, roll up in a beautiful carriage, knock on their magnificent manor house door, and announce who I am."

"Violet...what's goin' on in that devilish mind of yours?"

"*We* have to arrive on a really hot day, and you'll be in your trousers and hat! *Only* your trousers and hat."

"Darlin', you're jokin', right?"

"Not really," she exclaimed, then laughed and rolled her eyes. "I think my parents would absolutely love it."

"You are such a bad girl."

"Uh-huh, and you wouldn't want me any other way. Do you feel better now?"

"Yep."

"Good, because I have some other exciting news. I've just been waiting for the right time to tell you."

"I'm listenin'."

"Cooper, we need to turn that second bedroom into a nursery."

"You...you...we...are havin' a baby?"

"We are! I think it's why I've been so emotional lately. Don't you see? You and me and the family we're about to become, that's the real treasure we've been given."

Moving his arms around her, he hugged her tightly and fought back the happy tears.

"Darlin', the day I married you was the happiest day of my life, but I'm thinkin' this just might top it. Dang. Don't move, I'll be right back."

He was only gone a moment, and when he returned he was carrying something in his hand.

"What is that?"

"The day you arrived I sat down to whittle. You know how I do that?"

"Sure."

"Strange thing. I'd never carved a cat before, haven't since. Here," he said softly, handing her the beautifully crafted animal. "The first present for our little one, made on the day we met, and if it's a girl, I think we should call her Rose."

"This is perfect," she murmured, moving her fingers over the smooth wood, "and so is that name, but what if it's a boy?"

"Hamilton! What else?"

"Of course. Cooper, I love you so much it hurts."

"Me too," he said with a heavy breath "My beautiful Princess."

"Your wife. That's the only title I want or need."

THE END

Dear Reader:

Thank you for buying this book. If you have a moment I would greatly appreciate your review. I constantly strive to bring you interesting and enjoyable content and your feedback is valued. Feel free to contact me at any time. I love to hear from readers. My email is: MagCarpenter@yahoo.com, and here are my social media links should you care to check them out.
My very best wishes,
Maggie

---

http://www.MaggieCarpenter.com
https://www.facebook.com/MaggieCarpenterWriter
FOR A COMPLETE CATALOGUE OF MAGGIE'S BOOKS GO TO
Amazon.com/author/maggiecarpenter[1]
TO JOIN MAGGIE'S MAILING LIST AND GET A FREE BOOK GO TO
MaggieCarpeter.com[2]

---

1. http://Amazon.com/author/maggiecarpenter

2. http://MaggieCarpeter.com